—THE—
PROMISED

—LAND—

THE PROMISED LAND

A NOVEL

MARTIN WAXMAN

© Martin Waxman, 1987

Published by Black Moss Press in March 1987 with the assistance of the Canada Council and the Ontario Arts Council.

Black Moss Press books are distributed in Canada and the U.S. by Firefly Books.

ISBN 0-88753-160-1

Acknowledgements: Special thanks to Marty Gervais, Maureen Judge, Judith Fitzgerald, Lionel Koffler, the Ontario Arts Council, Maureen Paxton and Rod Willmot.

Cover design by Maureen Paxton.

To anyone who ever
worked in,
shopped at,
or passed through
The Fabric Center

*I've been many things at many times,
buildings large and small,
a bridge of steel, a catacomb...
Today I am a mall.*

— *Voice of Garden Park*

PHASE 1

1

Everyday at 11:30, Martin Mall felt the need to browse. He tried to overcome it, tried to freeze-dry the urge, but like an addict, he was hooked.

So everyday he'd leave his office, take the stairway down to the main level and wander over to the Republic Cigar Kiosk.

"Blue Trident, please," he'd say to the young girl behind the counter. He'd hand her a crumpled dollar bill and tell her to keep the change.

"No really, I can't," she'd say to Martin.

But despite her many protests, he'd always insist. A few minutes later Martin would reappear, this time to buy a newspaper.

"I won't take any more money from you," the young girl would say.

"Why not?" he'd ask her.

And before she could bat an eyelash, a quarter was resting in the palm of her hand.

The young girl reluctantly acquiesced. She'd smile at Martin. He'd grin back. She was only 15 and didn't want to make too much of a fuss.

"See you tomorrow," he'd say and disappear into the mall.

Martin had a crush on the young girl behind the counter. He liked her ... from the waist up. He never really got to know her bottom half. It was hidden by rows of magazines and candy. Once he noticed her walking through the mall on a break and barely recognized her. Seeing her as a complete entity with boots and legs that moved, made her a stranger to Martin. And although this upset him (he actually gave up gum for a week), it was hardly an unusual phenomenon. He had the same trouble placing bank tellers without windows, sales clerks without counters or cashiers without bagboys.

"Why can't people just stick to their context?" he complained to his secretary, Peaches del Muhne.

"That's their business, not yours," Peaches replied.

The ritual continued.

Martin said hello to everyone he passed: to staff and managers, serious and casual customers, customers with bags, sons and daughters of customers, customers with blank stares, customers with blank cheques and on and on and on...

On busy days his greetings were transformed into one long atonal ahhhhhhh. He didn't want to leave anyone unacknowledged. He convinced himself it was his duty, as manager of Garden Park, to make every single person feel at home there, regardless of race, creed or credit limit.

Even when he had a throat infection and couldn't talk for a week, Martin wouldn't allow himself the luxury of a missed day. Instead he bought a conventioneer's "hello, my name is..." stick-on label, filled in his moniker, displayed it proudly on his lapel and strutted through the mall — nodding at everyone and pointing to his badge. The Merchants' Association misinterpreted his action. They took it as a policy position. By that afternoon over half of the retailers were sporting name tags of their own. Caught up in the frenzy, many of the customers also joined in. And for a while, it looked as though Garden Park was about to become a first-name basis mall. But as the adhesive dried, so did the enthusiasm. And Martin's voice returned.

The name tags were dropped. Not without a round of self-congratulations, though and a pledge to continue it next year as a 2-day event. The Merchants' Association honored Martin's good-will gesture with a citation of thanks, which he was only too happy to place alongside the other framed plaques on the wall in his office.

No doubt about it, Martin Mall had leadership tendencies.

"It isn't often," said Calvin Dighby, president of the Merchants' Association, "that a mall manager takes an interest in anything outside of sidewalk sales and maintenance fees. Martin's different. He's a man of the people."

"He understands good shopping," said Susan Carlyle. "Like we all do," she added quickly.

"He's a minor celebrity in a major retail development," Edgar Portlee chimed in.

These are all direct quotes from Garden Park's bi-monthly newsletter. Editor: Martin Mall.

2

Sandy Rodd was a born-again salesperson. Actually, she was quite a bit more than that. She'd recently been promoted to Vice-President in charge of Creative Expansion for the Sheer Curtains drapery chain.

Not a bad title for a 28-year-old, whose only notable accomplishment had been working for her father as a glorified sales clerk. Now she was employed by a large conglomerate as a glorified executive; a retail dream come true.

But that wasn't always the case. Sandy remembered the time when she hated working, abhorred selling and literally despised customers. (She was always making comments under her breath.) She seriously considered packing it in for law or a career in the arts.

She described this as her rebellious period.

She spent many sleepless nights toying with the idea of ripping the draperies off all her windows. She even went as far as buying a pair of pinking sheers, which she kept sharpened and hidden in the bottom of her underwear drawer. She came close, too; the symmetry of the pleats being the only thing that stopped her. Who knows where Sandy would be today, if she didn't surround herself with fabrics of quality and style?

Then one Saturday, quite unexpectedly, Sandy Rodd met her maker. It was late, almost closing time. She was in the store, doing very well and resenting every minute of it. All of a sudden she began to feel faint. And she did something quite unusual, she turned a customer over to a junior clerk before the order had been signed. She excused herself, walked to the office, closed the door and collapsed at the desk.

She was awakened by the sounds of a cash register symphony. The music was soothing and calm. It called to her in a language that spoke true to her heart.

"Follow me," it was saying, "follow me."

"Where to?" she asked.

"Katchukitachukitachuk," it answered. "Ding. Beep."

That was all Sandy needed to hear.

She felt herself rising through the roof of her store and high above the mall. She let herself be carried to a secluded showroom in the far end of an industrial park. The warehouse was filled with hundreds of pairs of custom-made drapes, each set more beautiful than the one before. Sandy admired the workmanship. There is a God, she thought.

"Hello," said a man. "I have something for you."

He startled Sandy. She hadn't heard him come in. It took her a second to regain her composure.

"Oh really," she replied. "What is it?"

"Just this." He smiled as he handed her a pair of silk stockings. "Try them on. They're the real thing."

Sandy was puzzled. "You must have the wrong person," she said to the stranger. "These can't be for me."

The man shook his head. "Afraid you're mistaken Sandy Rodd, these are definitely for you."

"You — you know my name. How do you know my name? Who told you my name?"

"They say you have the gift, Sandy Rodd. They say you have the perfect pitch. Don't squander it. You are one of the chosen."

Her face was ashen. "Who chose me?" she pleaded.

The man was silent. His task was complete. He turned away from her and slowly walked toward the curtains. They parted and swallowed him up. Sandy watched him disappear, wondering who he was, searching for even the faintest glimmer of recognition.

She looked at the stockings. She tried them on. A card fell out of the box and onto the floor. "A salesman's got to dream," it read. "It goes with the territory."

"Oh my god. That was him. That was.... That was... Willy... Come back Willy," she called to the silence. "Don't leave me. Please don't go."

She opened her eyes. She scanned the tiny office. Everything was right where it should be. I must have been dreaming she thought. That's it, dreaming.

Just then she noticed the silk stockings. Sandy began to cry. Each tear brought her closer to the stranger, closer to reality, closer to herself. And for one fleeting moment, the universe became crystal clear. Sandy experienced truth with a capital T.

"Everything is selling," she repeated to herself. "Selling is everything..."

Her pilgrimage was complete. Sandy Rodd had been born again.

3

Garden Park was only half a mall. But it was in the process of becoming whole again. It was going to be 25 years old and every mall which reached that milestone, just like every human being who spent the same amount of time with a single employer, was entitled to its just reward.

In Garden Park's case, that gold watch was a major facelift. Not just on the inside, but structurally, too. The exterior stucco was being upgraded, replaced by amber brick, the tile floors recovered in marble, the roof literally raised off it beams to make way for the addition of a second level. Skylights and incandescents would replace the old fluorescents. There would soon be an enclosed parking area and each store was to have a new look of its own. The existing mall was being used as a famework, a coat of primer, the underbelly of the beast.

If a future archaeologist happened to discover the ruins of the New Garden Park, say in 1000 years and if they continued to dig a bit deeper, they would no doubt conclude that a more advanced civilization must have destroyed the remnants of its inferior. This was exactly what the designers were hoping to achieve.

So Garden Park was 2/3 finished and the mall was an absolute mess. Only about 2 dozen of the 171 (soon to be 246) stores bothered to remain open during the renovations. The rest of the retailers took their rent and percentage rebates and pretended they were in showbiz: arriving at all hours, obsessed with their project, hyping elaborate plans.

It was not a shopper's haven. But Garden Park had a very loyal following. These were customers who, like Martin Mall, could not for any reason alter their shopping ritual. And rather than interrupting their biological clocks they gathered at the mall, every single day, and were content to mill around, watching the contruction and commenting on the progress.

The current attraction, the installation of the marble floor, was the biggest crowd pleaser to date. The workers labored behind a fenced-off barricade, giving their task a circus-like appeal. And each time a new chunk was set down, the appreciative audience burst into applause.

As if on cue, this happened when Martin Mall was walking by and, mistaking the applause for himself, he bowed very low and began to make a speech. It didn't take him long to realize that the accolades weren't meant for him. But he didn't care. He considered himself interchangeable with his mall.

Martin ambled on, spending longer than usual on his mid-morning stroll. And with good reason. He was psyching himself up for an encounter with a new retailer. Not an easy task for someone who believed the venerable reputation of the mall he managed hinged on his every word and deed.

That was why he made an extra stop at the Republic Cigar Kiosk for a second flavor of gum.

"Not everyone likes blue," he said to the young girl behind the counter, who could do little else but agree. "At least this way I can offer Sandy Rodd the freedom of choice."

"Who's Sandy Rodd?" the young girl asked, not that she cared.

Martin didn't hear her. "Freedom of choice," he added, "that's the mandate of malls."

He paused for a moment, then reached inside his pocket, took out a small pad of paper and wrote down his pith. He had a feeling it would come in handy one day. He didn't want to lose it.

4

It was her first day in Garden Park and Sandy Rodd was less than impressed. For one thing her store was a shambles, for another so was the mall. Why didn't anyone tell her they were in the middle of a structural revision? She would have postponed her grand opening at least another week. Now she would have to do some fancy explaining to head office.

Sandy Rodd hated justification.

And to make matters worse, in the 2 hours since she'd arrived, not one retailer had even waved or walked by. Where was the Merchants' Association welcoming committee, she wondered. What kind of a mall was this?

Sandy felt very alone.

Her eyes darted anxiously around the clutter, making mental notes of everything that had to be done — if only that phone would stop ringing...

Martin Mall was still clutching his pad of paper when he reached the Sheer Curtains outlet. He stood there silently, waiting for Sandy to finish her call.

"...Yes, Seymour ...Yes, Seymour ...They're ordered, Seymour ...It's all taken care of ...What? No-yes, I mean. It really is starting to take shape. You're acting like this is the first time I've ...Of course I can handle it..."

Martin cleared his throat as politely as possible. Sandy looked up. It took her a moment to focus in on him. He was standing so quietly she thought he might be a mannequin. But Sandy Rodd knew she'd never seen a mannequin with a grin like that.

She nodded to Martin. His smile grew even wider. Since this was her first time in Garden Park, she didn't recognize Martin Mall. She mistook him for an overly eager customer.

Sandy held up a finger. "I'll be with you in a minute," she said, sizing him up. "Seymour, I've got to run. Someone just came in. I know we're not open, but I'm telling you, a little advance PR never hurt anybody. See you next week, OK? ...I will. I promise. Bye."

Sandy took a deep breath. "Welcome to my nightmare," she said, gesturing to the state of the store. "Although you must admit, it's no worse than out there in the mall."

That stung. Martin took it as a personal insult.

"I hope you'll forgive the mess," she continued, "but our grand opening isn't till next Thursday. That doesn't mean you can't place an order right now if you see something that strikes your fancy."

Sandy was always ready to sell a pair of drapes. Anywhere. Anytime. Anyhow. She even carried a trunkload of samples in her car and couldn't leave a party without first selling at least one set of sheers. Her father was proud. Not only had he raised a daughter, but a damn good salesperson, too.

"Actually," Martin said, "I'm just looking..."

His cliché made them both wince. He regretted it immediately. He wished he could have been more inventive, maybe referred to his notebook. Still, he didn't want to introduce himself yet. A few more minutes playing customer and he would be able to gauge what percentage of the gross this store would bring to the mall.

"That's funny," Sandy segued, digging into a carton. "I was looking for something before you came in; the box with our lagniappes."

"I beg your pardon."

"I'm sorry," she replied. "I didn't mean to get technical. Lagniappes are small gifts we give away to customers, little curtained windows in your choice of sheer or antique satin. They make exceptional wall hangings. Perhaps you'd like one?"

She rummaged through a different crate and pulled out...

"Well, what do you know," she said, half to herself.

"Is that a lagniappe?" Martin asked her.

"No," said Sandy, only slightly patronizing. "This is an order book." She pointed to the first page. "See? Number 00001." She paused. "That could be you. You could be Sheer Curtains in Garden Park's founding customer. It's quite an achievement, you know. You get a membership card and updates on the latest drapery news. It also entitles you to a lifetime discount."

"I've never been a founding customer before," Martin lied. "Usually I like to wait till a store has established itself before giving it any of my business."

"A trendsetter like you?"

Martin mistook her pitch for a genuine compliment. "Thank you," he mumbled.

"I bet you'd be interested in our newest lines. Now what colors did you say you were matching?"

I didn't, thought Martin. Sandy Rodd was very smooth.

"Is it for your family room?"

"Excuse me," he said. "I have a confession to make. I'm not interested in drapes. I'm Martin Mall."

Sandy recognized the name.

"I'm sorry for the little charade," he continued, "I've heard so much about your work. I just wanted a chance to see you in action. I must say, I was very impressed with your technique."

Sandy was flattered, but she refused to let Martin off the hook. It was against her principles to give up, once she had the scent of a customer in her veins.

Before long she had given him an estimate of what it would cost to re-do his office with inherently fire-retardant mod-acrylic. "Very post-60s," she said. "It's all the rage." Sandy told him that his drapes would take top priority, that she would personally measure his windows and that a 6 to 10 week delivery was guaranteed.

"All this," said Martin, "and you don't install?"

A look of anguish appeared on her face. "Board of Directors' decision," she replied, "not mine."

For a moment there was an uncomfortable silence.

"Would you like a piece of gum?" Martin earnestly held out the two packs. "Freedom of choice," he said, "the mandate of malls."

"No thanks," Sandy answered. "I don't chew."

"I had no idea," said Martin. "Well, I guess I'd better be going. It's already after noon. I'm sure I'll see you around the neighborhood."

Sandy sensed she was losing the sale and readied herself for one final assault. "Wait — I mean, say is there anyplace good to eat around here?"

"Are you kidding? Garden Park has 42 dining establishments. Although right now..." his tone became apologetic, "only 3 are operational."

"Please go on," she said.

"Well, you could eat where staff eats, at Grant Drugs' lunch counter; where management eats, at Cappy's Seafood Emporium; or you could venture to neutral territory and gaze at the mall through the eyes of pancakes."

"Pancakes sound fine to me. Now is this my treat or yours?"

"Wait a minute. Are we having lunch. Nobody said anything about lunch?"

"I just thought, being new here and all..."

"You certainly work fast."

"In my business you have to."

"Then I think this lunch should be on you," he said, "considering the money we may be laying out for that new set of drapes."

"I'll buy that," Sandy replied. "Just let me get my steel tape. I never go anywhere without it."

"Don't forget my lagniappe," Martin called after her.

"I won't..."

And Sandy smiled. As far as she was concerned, this sale was as good as money in the bank.

5

Madame Alice's Pancake Palace was buzzing with activity. Every table was full, with retailers and designers exchanging concepts over coffee and crepes. There was a lineup to get in. Each time the hostess passed by people shouted, "We've got a 3 here," or "Can't you squeeze us into that booth?" or "How much longer do I have to wait? I only get a 2-hour lunch."

Martin led Sandy to the front of the line. "Hello Mr. Mall," the hostess said. "We have your usual table."

"A regular," said Sandy. "I'm impressed."

Martin motioned to her. "You go ahead. I have to do something."

"Me too. Which way is the ladies room?"

When she returned, Sandy was struck by the energy of the Palace. It felt as if everyone in the restaurant knew each other and were in the middle of a private party. She looked through the crowd for a familiar face, someone to say, "Hi Sandy. Care to join us?" But she was like an immigrant, fresh off the boat; a stranger, and they sensed it. I do not exist in this mall, she thought. I am a non-entity. She opened her purse and fingered her business cards. All that's going to change starting now.

Martin joined Sandy, stopping to greet at least 10 or 12 people along the way. He was carrying a plaque, a plastic replica of the one which hung over the cash register. It contained a pancake being flipped high in the air and the inscription, "Lunch means never having to say you're hungry." He handed it to Sandy.

"Can a non-retailer like me, give a retailer like you a lagniappe?" He was only half kidding.

"Technically no," she replied. "Unless it's a pen or a calendar, something with your name on it. But thanks just the same."

"What about this?" He was referring to the "reserved exclusively for Martin Mall" sign that was permanently affixed to the centerpiece of the table. "I had it commissioned."

"That's closer..."

"You probably think I'm just plain ignorant," said Martin.

"Not at all," she said, "Naive maybe. Retail is a multifaceted discipline, not something you can pick up off the street."

He was about to mention his experience in the mall, when they were interrupted by their waitress.

"Will there be anything else?" she asked.

He shook his head.

"I'd like a refill," said Sandy. "And by the way, I couldn't help admiring your drapes. How long have you had them?"

"Beats me," said the waitress. "I've only been here 5 years. You want me to ask the manager?"

"That won't be necessary," Sandy replied. She took out a business card, scribbled something on the back and gave it to the waitress. "See that the manager gets this," she said.

The waitress examined the card, moving her lips as she read: "Sheer Curtains in Garden Park; 'When it comes to windows, we've got you covered'; Sandy Rodd, Vice-President, Creative Expansion."

"You're new here, aren't you?" she asked.

"We've just moved in."

"It's funny, my husband and I have been thinking of turning the twins' room into a den. Maybe we'll drop by and look for some drapes. Do you sell verticals, too?"

"The works," said Sandy. And she took out another card. "This entitles you to a 10% discount."

"Thank you," said the waitress. "Thank you very much." She poured them each a fresh cup of coffee and slipped them extra creams. "Friday's my day off. You can expect me then." She gave Sandy a conspiratorial wink. "No charge for these. They're on the house."

Martin waited until the waitress was out of earshot before he spoke. "Do you always give your card out so indiscriminately?" There was a touch of annoyance in his voice.

"I'm networking," said Sandy. "Is that a crime?"

"Around here," Martin replied, "that can get you into very serious trouble."

He went on to explain that by giving the waitress a discount card, Sandy had violated the Garden Park Shopping Code, which stated that management was allocated a 15% discount off any item purchased in the mall, a professional courtesy, so to speak. Staff, on the other hand, was only allowed a discount in their place of employment and even then it was strictly at the discretion of their employers.

"It's not that we're trying to tread on the masses. It's simply a question of ethics. If everyone got the same discount what would be the point of being a manager? Of course, you and I know the answer to that. Being a manager is its own reward. But working people need something to strive for."

Edgar Portlee came up from behind. "There you are," he said. "I've been looking all over for you. Your office told me I might find you here... Oh, I'm sorry... I hope I'm not intruding..."

"Actually," said Martin, "we were right in the middle of..."

"Won't you join us," Sandy interjected.

She's networking again, thought Martin.

"I don't want to impose," said Edgar.

"It's no imposition," Sandy replied.

"In that case..." Edgar pulled up a chair and was looking at the menu, before Martin had a chance to make the introductions.

"Edgar," Martin said, "I'd like you to meet Sandy Rodd."

She held out her hand.

"I'm Edgar Portlee," he said. "Glad to know you. Say, you wouldn't happen to be related to a Harry Rodd, would you?"

"I certainly am," she replied. "He's my dad."

"Well, what do you know," said Edgar. "It sure is a small world."

They all agreed that it was.

"I'm an old friend of your father's," Edgar said.

Sandy was about to reach for her card, when Edgar beat her to the punch.

"Edgar is President and General Manager of Portlee Inc. Designatore," Martin said. "Just down the mall."

"The store for overweight women," Edgar said, beaming.

Sandy stared at his card. It was small and round and stuffed with quilting. It reminded her of Edgar's cheeks. Under Edgar's name was written the company credo: "The bigger the bustle, the harder we hustle."

"I wrote it myself," said Edgar, proudly. "So tell me Sandy Rodd, daughter of my good buddy Harry, what brings you to Garden Park?"

"What brings anyone to any mall," she said. And before Martin could say, "We've just done a survey on that very subject," Sandy answered: "We're opening a Sheer Curtains."

"Another one?" Edgar was stunned.

"What can I tell you? Business is good."

"Then how come you're so skinny?" Edgar asked her.

"I didn't realize you worked for your father," Martin said.

"Actually, I work with him."

"Attagirl," said Edgar. "Keep the old man on his toes."

"You're really lucky," said Martin. "I always wanted to work with my father."

"So why didn't you?" Sandy asked.

Martin was silent.

"Don't tell me," said Edgar. "He wasn't in retail, right? So what was he? A dentist? ...A professional?"

"Stop it Edgar, please," Martin said. "You know I never met him."

"I'm sorry," said Sandy.

"Quit your bellyaching," said Edgar. "If you came to work for me, like I asked you maybe a hundred times, I would've treated you better than family."

"I couldn't leave the mall, Edgar."

"You would've still been here."

"It's not the same," Martin said.

"He thinks he's too good for retail. I don't know why we're having lunch with him." Edgar took a long contemplative breath. "I'm really sorry I lost touch with your father, Sandy. I haven't seen him in over 20 years. We used to be in business together. A carwash. But I guess that's water under the bridge." Edgar chuckled at his levity. "You think old Harry would mind if I called him sometime?"

"You don't have to," Sandy said. "You can see him in person. He's flying in for our grand opening."

"Son of a gun," said Edgar. "He hasn't lost it yet."

"I'll tell him I met you."

"I'd rather you didn't," Edgar said. "Let this be our little secret, OK?"

"No problem. By the way ... if you're ever interested in drapes." Sandy handed Edgar her card.

He accepted it graciously. "A chip off the old block," he said. "I don't know how much more of this I can take. Sandy, it was a pleasure meeting you. It's time for me to head back."

"Wait a minute," Sandy said. "Didn't you come here to see Martin Mall?"

Edgar searched his short term memory. "I suppose I did," he replied. "I forgot all about it."

"So?" said Sandy.

"So what?" said Edgar.

"So what did you come to see Martin about?"

"It's not important," said Edgar.

"It must be something," said Sandy.

"We can discuss it another day."

"If it's man-talk I can leave."

Edgar blushed. "It's nothing like that," he said. "I just had an idea for Martin's television show."

"You have your own show?" she said to Martin. "I had no idea I was dining with such a celebrity."

"I'm sorry. What?" said Martin. He was so mesmerized by Sandy and Edgar's verbal ping pong match, that he lost track of their conversation.

"Your TV show," said Sandy.

"Oh," said Martin. "It's not really a show yet. It's..."

"Just a pilot," Edgar interjected. "It premieres on Garden Park's 25th anniversary and the Grand Reopening of the mall."

"Sounds exciting," Sandy said. "What kind of program is it?"

"A talk show," Edgar replied. "What else?"

"Does it have a title?"

"Shop Talk."

"Where's it being taped?"

"In front of the garden in the middle of the mall," Edgar said. "It's the perfect location."

"So where do we fit in?" Sandy asked. Sandy was trying to exist with a vengeance.

"Can *I* say something?" Martin was almost surprised to hear his own voice. "After all, it is my..."

"Be my guest," Edgar said. "No one's stopping you... That's a good one. You're the host and I tell you to be my guest."

"I'd love to see the pilot sometime," Sandy said.

Edgar looked at his calendar. "How about this afternoon?"

"Fine with me," she said.

"Good. Then it's settled," he replied.

Sandy smiled. Edgar laughed. Martin sighed.

"Waitress," Edgar called.

"Yes customer," she answered.

"Another round of pancakes for my table." He winked at Sandy. "We're going to get you into my clothes, yet."

6

Peaches del Muhne was operating in a tizzy when Martin brought Sandy and Edgar into his office, unannounced.

"Mister," she said, "You've got a lot of nerve. You knew full well you had an appointment to screen the pilot for the Merchants' executive. They waited for over an hour then left in a huff. And I don't blame them either. I would've done the same." She eyed Sandy. "And what are you doing bringing in guests without consulting me first? You're violating my sense of organization. I'll tell you one thing Martin Mall, you've certainly mastered the art of ruining my afternoons... Oh hello Edgar."

"Hello Peaches," Edgar said. "Your coat will be ready at the end of the week. The alterations are almost done."

"Thank you Edgar... Well," she said to Martin, "what do you have to say for yourself?"

"I'm sorry Peaches, but some things are bigger than datebooks."

"Name one," she said.

Martin couldn't think of any.

"See," she replied.

"Peaches," said Martin, "I'd like you to meet Sandy Rodd."

"A pleasure," she said, coolly.

"Sandy, Edgar and I have an important meeting, so I'd appreciate it if you'd hold my calls, especially if it's the Merchants' Association. I don't want to deal with them right now."

"Hold your own calls," she snapped. "I'm your secretary, not your doormat. Don't tread on me..."

They entered Martin's inner office.

"..And another thing..." Peaches continued her tirade on the intercom, which Martin proceeded to shut off.

"You'll have to forgive Peaches," he said. "She's really a wonderful secretary. She just can't tolerate spontaneous behavior. It's her upbringing — third generation bureaucrat."

"Will she be OK?" Sandy asked. "Maybe we should leave."

"No, no, no," Martin replied. "She'll be fine in a minute. So sit down and make yourselves comfortable. Can I get you anything?"

"Bicarbonate of soda," said Edgar. "I think I had one pancake too many."

"One bicarb coming up. Sandy?"

"Nothing for me," she said.

"You sure?"

Sandy was positive. She was too busy drinking in the condition of the room. The stained rug, drab furnishings, tacky awards (arranged chronologically) and, best of all, worn out drapes were quenching Sandy's thirst like no liquid ever could. I've got my work cut out for me, she thought. Too bad I'm not into office interiors.

"Before we begin," Martin said. "I want you to realize that what you're about to see has never been shown to retailers before. You may be overwhelmed. It's a groundbreaking premise, conceptually original in every way — although I will admit that some of my inspiration came from the Jerry Lewis Telethon."

"Beautiful guy," said Edgar. "We could all take a lesson."

Martin was convinced Edgar already had.

"Any questions?" he asked. "No? Then I guess we're ready."

He dimmed the lights and turned on the VCR. Sandy and Edgar looked on in anticipation.

The show opened almost professionally — with a theme song, a violin and harp arrangement of Rick Nelson's "Garden Party"; followed by a quick cut montage, so frenzied in motion, it felt like the cameras went temporarily insane. When the picture finally stabilized, in front of an empty, darkened set, the voice of an announcer echoed through the mall: "Attention shoppers, we have a lost little boy, waiting to be claimed — by each and every one of you! I'd like to bring him on now, the star of our show — Mr. Shopping Center himself... Let's really hear it for Martin Mall..."

The muzak swelled, as much as muzak can. Then the lights came up, Martin appeared on stage and the audience burst into applause.

So did Sandy and Edgar. It seemed like the right thing to do.

Martin grinned at the camera and waited for the ovation to die down. He gestured to his set, which was designed by a team of 6 window dressers. Every piece of furntiure had a price tag and sign, telling you where each item could be bought.

"It's all for sale," said Martin. "How 'bout a hand for our Merchants' Association. They deserve it... Thank you. Welcome to our show. It's great to be back in Garden Park, although quite frankly, I can't remember the last time I left. So how're you all doing? Don't forget, it's payday tomorrow..."

At the mention of money, the crowd re-burst into applause.

"Save it for the bank," he said. He was really on a roll. "Anyway, back to business. You know, this is our first foray into the world of entertainment. Not that shopping isn't entertaining... I wanna tell ya, I wouldn't trade it for the world. Not even for a Pontiac..."

Martin paused and stared blankly at the camera, waiting for the response that never came. It took him a moment to regain his composure.

"But seriously," he said. "We're going to introduce our first guest — someone you'll be seeing as a regular on our program — here is the Wandering Customer."

"Wandering Customer," said Sandy. "That's cute."

Martin was hurt. "It's more than that."

"I meant it as a compliment."

"Maybe you should watch and save your compliments till the end."

There was a sale in the offing so Sandy bit her tongue and returned her attention to the screen. She saw the image from a shaky, moving camera. It traversed the long main corridor of the mall, slowing down occasionally, to glance and almost nod at window displays or back-lit logos. It stopped in front of Prime Jeans, went inside, and inspected the first few racks of clothing.

"May I help you?" asked a salesclerk, who was staring directly into the lens.

"Yes," said a voice from behind the camera. "I'm looking for some steel blue corduroys."

"What size?"

"32 long," came the reply.

The salesclerk politely showed the camera different styles of pants, until a suitable pair was chosen.

"I'll take these."

"That'll be $19.95 plus tax." The salesclerk rang up the sale and put the newly purchased item in a bag. She thanked the camera with a variation of the standard "have a nice day." "Have a wonderful day," she said.

"You too," said the voice.

Just as the camera was about to leave, it focused on the store's logo, and the announcer said, "Prime Jeans... cords and tops, too. Designer is our middle name."

Where was the manager? Sandy wondered. And how can they sleep at night knowing their business' reputation was in the hands of a salesclerk?

No doubt about it, this was the mark of an outsider. Sandy always knew when a person wasn't born to retail.

The Wandering Customer continued down the mall, stopped for soda and then entered Penny Lane Hair Design. He zoomed in on a reclining Martin.

"Let's hear it for the Wandering Customer," he said. "I can't wait to see what he's bought... Well, we're back and I'm in the number one chair of Penny Lane Hair Design, with Calvin Dighby, doing what he does best."

"Could you please hold still," said an irritated Calvin. "Otherwise the whole thing will be lopsided."

"You mean like last time?" Martin was attempting an ad lib.

Calvin was not amused. "One more snip," he said, "and we'll be done. There." He held up a mirror. "Is that art!?"

Martin was about to answer when Calvin reached for a Polaroid and snapped Martin's picture. While it was developing, Martin suggested that he pull out his album. Calvin graciously obliged.

"Tell us about it," Martin said.

"Gladly. Drawing on my mentors, those 4 mop-topped lads from Liverpool — who changed the face of hair design forever — I take a photograph..." (He sang the rest.) "...of every head I have the pleasure to know. La, la, la, la, la, la, la..." A tear trickled down his cheek. "Forgive me. But if it weren't for them and especially Ringo, I would probably have gone into banking." Calvin was all choked up.

"So... why do you take the pictures?" Martin was searching for a segue.

Calvin blew his nose.

"Calvin..."

"I don't know what's come over me," he said. "I've got the shivers. Maybe it's all these lights."

"The pictures..."

"Oh yes," he said, pulling himself together. "It's just so touching, that's all. Anyway, as I started to tell you, I keep a photographic record of every head that passes through my portals. I like going back to a person's roots. Actually, it started out as a hobby, but it's grown into something much bigger. I'm having it published."

"No kidding," said Martin. "What's the title?"

"The book will be called 'A Pictorial Hairstory — by Calvin Dighby.' It's a social comment."

"I'll be looking for it."

"You won't have to look hard. I'm distributing it myself. You know, if I may be so bold, I'd like to mention my last chapter, which has some startling predictions about what the future will bring..."

"Sounds like it's ahead of its time," Martin chuckled.

Calvin glared at him. "Don't mock me," he said. He picked up his album and stormed off-screen.

"I think we should bring on our next guest..." Martin said. And he was back on the stage of his main set, noticeably trimmed and coiffed. "...a gentleman," he continued without missing a beat, ::who's just completed a fantastic 30% off special. He's currently working on a buy 1, get 1 free sale. Ladies and Gentlemen, please give a warm, warm welcome to Edgar Portlee..."

"That's me," said Edgar, nearly falling off his chair. "That's me. Hey, I don't look so bad on TV, do I?"

"On the contrary," said Sandy. "You're a natural."

"Shhh..." said Martin.

"Last time I work for whole-scale," Edgar said.

"So Edgar," said Martin, on the show, "nice of you to drop by."

"Last time I work for whole-scale," said Edgar, on-screen. The audience tittered appreciatively. Edgar had a reputation as a kidder.

"What's this I hear about your having a 2 for 1 sale?" Martin asked.

"Hear nothing," Edgar replied. "Seeing is believing." He held up a glossy 4 page flier. "Can you get a close-up of this beauty?"

Edgar and Martin chatted for a little while longer, then Edgar excused himself, explaining that he had signs to put up.

And just when it seemed like the pilot was over, after Martin thanked everyone for appearing, he said, "Ladies and gentlemen, was this a bargain?" The audience signalled their approval. "Good. I'm glad you agree. And with a little luck, we'll be here, every day, 6 days a week, for much more of the same. Is that a fitting way to kick off Garden Park's Grand Reopening and 25th Anniversary or what? And now, it's time for our big finish — or should I say, our new beginning. Listen. We're in the process of installing roving cameras all around Garden Park. They will follow you, as you go about your business, from the moment we open in the morning, until the moment we close at night. You will all get a chance to be guests on my show. My friends, you are the Wandering Customers! and you... and you... and you..."

The crowd swooned as the cameras swished around them.

"I agree," he said. "It is exciting."

Martin then removed the cover from a large object that was looming in the background and revealed a giant, 3-dimensional cash register. The keys contained the names of every store in the mall.

"There's more," he continued, "so much more. This is no ordinary machine." His voice was shaking. "This is the missing link. The key that will unite us — retailers, customers and management alike — into one inalienable whole. Let me explain. Each time you buy an item, the money you spend and the store where you made your purchase will be flashed up here and on TV screens all over the mall. Now multiply that one sale exponentially and add a soundtrack of 1001 cash registers ringing simultaneously. Are you with me? Yes, you are beginning to comprehend our greater shopping consciousness. From this day forth, we share the pleasure of consumption. Everyone shops together, no one shops alone. ONE IS THE MALL! THE MALL IS ONE! This is my anniversary present to you and Garden Park!"

At Martin's signal, the machine burst into life with dancing numbers, high strung blips and frantic bells.

A cash register symphony... Sandy Rodd had deja vu.

The audience, reacting as they would to a fireworks display, responded with glee.

Martin stood there, with his cash register and his concepts and bowed very low. The lights dimmed and the show came to a close.

It all fits together, thought Sandy. I underestimated Martin Mall. It will be an honor selling him a new set of drapes.

Martin switched off the VCR. "Well, what's your verdict?"

"It's perfect," said Sandy. "You've got a hit on your hands."

"Could I see the part with me, again?" Edgar asked, only half in jest.

"You really like it. Honestly, I'm amazed. You're the first people I've shown this to, who wouldn't be biased, and you really liked it. I can't believe it." Martin was beginning to hyperventilate, "You work your whole life on an idea, a dream and by some miraculous twist of fate you live to see it happen, and it makes you so happy you just want to cry."

"So how do you feel right now?" Edgar asked.

"I feel like Merv," Martin replied.

He reached into his desk drawer and handed Sandy and Edgar each a cigar.

"Now that's a lagniappe," said Sandy.

"I know it's silly," Martin said.

"Nonsense," said Edgar. "It's your baby. I do the same thing, whenever I give birth to a new store. What about you, Sandy?"

"I go into a major depression."

Edgar examined the cigar. "These aren't the exploding kind?"

"They're from Cuba."

"That's what I mean." Edgar's comment brought their conversation to a halt. "Well, I'm glad I'm on your wavelength," he said.

"Pardon me," said Martin.

"My idea," he replied, "fits in perfectly with the format of your show."

"Oh," said Martin. "I forgot all about it."

"So do you want to hear it?" Edgar asked.

"I do," Sandy said.

Martin had no choice but to go along with the consensus.

Edgar began, "What we just saw was a variety show. And variety is, by its very definition, the spice of life. Am I right or wrong? Now, I don't mean anything personal by this, but imagining you up there as host every day, isn't exactly my idea of variety."

"Really," said Martin defensively. "What is?"

"Garden Park," he replied.

Martin couldn't argue. "I'll go along with that," he said.

"What I'm trying to say is you're running the show like a department store. If you ran it like the mall, there wouldn't only be one host. You might have dozens, even hundreds of MC's, each with their own special area of expertise. Get my drift? Look, with all my contacts and know-how, I'd be the perfect host for a fashion day. I could bring on my mannequins and demonstrate how overweight women in the audience could use their midriff bulge to look really stylish. Now, that's entertainment."

"Or," Sandy burst in, "I could conduct a question/answer period called 'Panel Talk', to help people solve their window decorating problems."

"Don't get me wrong," Edgar said. "I don't think you should give up hosting entirely. You could do it, maybe 2, 3 times a month and let us handle the rest. You'd still be the producer."

"Let me think about it," said Martin, who was no longer feeling like Merv.

"That's all I'm asking... partner."

Martin winced. I'm not imagining things, he thought. People are jealous. They really are trying to squeeze me out. Yet, by the same token, he couldn't help feeling Edgar had a point. "It's getting late," he said. "Maybe you'd better go. Besides, my head is pounding."

"I understand," said Edgar. "Over-stimulation."

"Thanks for showing us the pilot," Sandy said. "I hope you feel better."

"I just need some peace and quiet," Martin said. "I've got a lot on my mind."

Sandy and Edgar waved as they left.

"I never measured your windows," Sandy called back to him, "but don't worry, I haven't forgotten."

Martin sat down at his desk and rubbed his temples. "Peaches," he said into the intercom, "could you please bring in the first aid kit. I need some aspirin. Peaches... Peaches..."

When he got no response he went to the outer office. It was deserted. Peaches had left for the day. Martin walked over to her desk. It was immaculate as usual. He turned back toward his door and noticed a large manila envelope taped to it.

Martin opened the packet and found a long memo from Peaches. He decided to read it later. He glanced at the rest of the contents: 2 renewal contracts, some artwork to be approved and about a dozen phone messages, 7 from the Merchants' Association and the rest from a Seymour Black.

"Seymour Black," Martin said, "Seymour Black. That name sounds familiar."

But no matter how hard he tried, he just couldn't place it.

Just then the phone rang.

"Hello — Garden Park," said Martin.

"Martin Mall please."

"May I ask who's calling."

"Just tell him it's Seymour Black..."

7

Sandy returned to her store escorted by Edgar Portlee. On their way, she was approached by a young man in a plaid sports jacket with greasy blonde hair and too-wide lapels. He was almost handsome in a German shepherd sort of way. He stood quite erect in front of the photo booth. At first his come-on was so inaudible that Sandy asked him to repeat it.

"I said," he replied, increasing the movement in his lips but not his volume, "Take your picture with me for only $1.00. I'm very photogenic and you could show it to all your friends."

"No thank you," said Sandy.

"She's new here," Edgar said to him. "Try her next week. She'll come around."

When they were out of earshot, Sandy asked Edgar, "What do you mean I'll come around? I thought that guy was very rude."

"You mean Chris? He's a tradition around here. Everyone's had their photo with him. In terms of popularity, he rivals Santa Claus, except he has the ability to sustain it all year long. And he never upstages a client."

"Sounds sleazy," said Sandy.

"It's a living."

They reached Sheer Curtains in time to see her sign being installed. As if by remote control, the crowd that had earlier watched the progress of the new marble floor, gathered in front of her store to enjoy and partake in the proceedings. There were murmurs of oohs and ahhhs as a particular piece of plastic was set down and bolted in its rightful place. Avoiding her gut reaction, she refrained from passing out discount cards. Sandy wished she'd covered the sign with a theatrical curtain. Then, at the appropriate moment exposed it with a flourish. This would have served the double purpose of unveiling her sign as well as demonstrating the versatility of her product.

Making the best of things, Sandy said to the onlookers, "It's like launching a ship. And there'll soon be a sale."

"So where's the champagne?" Edgar asked. For some reason that struck him as funny. He started to giggle, then laughed convulsively. Hysterical, he walked back to his store. "I'm high on pancakes," he kept muttering to himself.

"Excuse me," said a man, wearing a heavy trenchcoat, bowler hat and mirrored sunglasses. "Are you Sandy Rodd?"

"Yes I am. Can I help you?"

"There are too many people out here," said a similarly attired woman. "Could we talk inside?"

"I'd prefer it," Sandy replied. "That's where my samples are." As she led the pair into Sheer Curtains, she wondered why they were identically dressed. Probably some kind of cult, she thought. Well, to each his own. Sandy didn't discriminate. As far as she was concerned, drapes belonged to the world.

"You'll have to excuse the mess," she said, "our grand opening isn't till next week..."

"It's OK," said the woman. "The coast is clear."

"I hope you'll forgive the secrecy, Ms. Rodd, but one can't be too careful these days. Let me make the introductions." They removed their sunglasses in unison. "I'm Calvin Dighby, President of the Merchants' Association..."

Sandy recognized him from the pilot.

"Pleased to meet you," she said.

"This is Susan Carlyle," he continued, "my first Vice-President. Susan is manager of Prime Jeans."

Sandy held out her hand. "This may be none of my business," she said, "but are you a newcomer to retail?"

"Not all of us have influential fathers," Susan replied. "I've worked very hard to get where I am."

"I'm sure we all have," Calvin said diplomatically. And he added to Susan, "Don't forget why we're here."

"Alright... We're here to officially welcome you to Garden Park," she said, with a touch of frost in her voice. She gave Sandy a copy of the Mall Family Tree, a gold embossed page of emergency phone numbers, suitable for framing. "Keep it next to your cash register. That's the way we do things around here."

"Thanks for the advice," said Sandy. "But half of the stores aren't open yet."

"It's for when they are," Susan answered. "We're not big on temporary solutions."

"I'm sorry there are only two of us," Calvin said. "I don't want you to get the wrong idea. We have lots of active members. They're just in hibernation — waiting for the Grand Reopening."

"Yes, of course," Sandy replied. "So... how much is it going to cost me to join?"

"I beg your pardon," said Calvin indignantly. "It won't cost you a dime."

"We're a non-profit organization," Susan said. "Membership is included in your rent."

"Then I guess I misjudged you," said Sandy. "I'm sorry. Look, why don't we start off on a new foot. Here's my card. It entitles you to a 10% discount. Now, may I take your coats?"

The wounded representatives shook their heads.

"Can we be frank, Ms. Rodd," Calvin said.

"Sure," said Sandy.

Susan pulled out a steno pad and began to read. "You arrived in Garden Park at 9:14 this morning — unaccompanied; at 11:47 you were paid an unexpected visit by a certain Martin Mall, which turned into lunch at Madame Alice's Pancake Palace, around 12:20. There, among other things, you presented a waitress with an unauthorized staff discount. We could have you thrown out of the Merchants' Association for that type of action. As it is, we're only going to slap your wrists — 6 months without a vote."

Sandy was impressed with Susan's clerical accuracy. "Were you ever a bookkeeper?" she asked.

"Yes," said Susan. "And I'm not ashamed to admit it. Shall I go on?"

"Why not?"

"At 1:14, your tête-a-tête became a ménage-à-trois, when Edgar Portlee joined your table. You left the restaurant just after 2:00 p.m. with Edgar and Martin, and the 3 of you were sequestered in Martin's office until 3:30 this afternoon."

"Were you following me?"

"Hardly."

"Then how do you know all this?" Sandy was experiencing a minor wave of paranoia.

"Malls have ears," said Calvin.

"The question is," Susan continued, "exactly how close are you to Martin Mall?"

"We've only met."

"Well you certainly work fast," said Susan.

"In my business..." Sandy stopped herself. Wait a minute, she thought, I'm not on trial. I haven't done anything wrong. "What are you getting at?" she asked.

"As I told you before," said Calvin, "one can't be too careful. We have to find out whose side you're on. We're in the middle of a war."

"Are you completely blind?" Susan asked. "We're here to discuss the future of Garden Park. Don't you see he's closing in on us?

Every moment draws us nearer to the end of retail as we know it. And it makes me sick to my stomach. I, for one, will not work under a totalitarian regime, where constant scrutiny and indiscriminate persecution are the specials of the day."

"Unless we stop him," Calvin picked up the gauntlet, "he'll destroy everything — our mall, our stores, our lives."

Sandy was stunned. This was the first truly reactionary Merchants' Association she had ever encountered. And one with uniforms, yet.

"Who are you talking about?" she asked.

"Who else?" Calvin replied. "Martin Mall."

"He's a megalomaniac," said Susan. "And I used to think that was a positive trait."

"Martin is a very unstable man..."

"That's not even his real name," Susan interrupted. "He used to be Martin Gray or White or some other color. But we gave him a new name. And we can take it away whenever we want."

"He has this pilot," Calvin continued.

"I know," said Sandy. "I saw it."

"We've been trying to screen it for weeks," said Calvin. "He avoids us. Can you at least empathize with the gravity of our situation?"

"Whose side are you on?" asked a belligerent Susan.

"My father warned me never to take sides," Sandy said. "It's poison for sales."

"I told you certain types of retail don't mix," Susan said to Calvin.

"Susan, relax," he said. "Have a little patience, please. Ms. Rodd... Sandy. Don't you realize that Martin's show impinges on our rights as independent business people? Remember the giant cash register?"

"Good concept," said Sandy.

"You're right," said Calvin, "it is. We have no real quarrel with the concept, just its execution. Did you know that Martin's machine is plugged into every one of our cash systems? And that at any given moment, it knows exactly how well we're doing?"

"Or how poorly," Susan added.

"Or how poorly," Calvin echoed. "He'll get the goods on us and we'll lose the last bit of leverage we had."

"It's the end of creative accounting," Susan prophesized glumly.

"Do you really think it's that bad?" Sandy asked.

"It's worse than price controls," Susan said. "Worse than the red scare."

"So what are you going to do?"

"Now you're talking," said Calvin. "The Merchants' Association is buying Garden Park."

"We're going condo," said Susan. "The whole world will be watching. Here. Read this."

She handed Sandy an untitled white report, prepared by the Merchants' Association executive. They had recently been to Quebec to study separatism and to Florida to learn the ins and outs of condominium development. They were not taking their task lightly.

"You might also want to look at this," said Calvin. He gave Sandy a copy of Garden Park's anniversary promotional booklet, The Birth of a Mall. "It never hurts to keep one step ahead of the enemy," he said.

"Remember," said Susan. "What we told you cannot go beyond this store."

"We'll keep you posted," said Calvin. "We'd better leave. OK Susan. Let's blow this pop stand."

"Wait," said Sandy. "Not yet. I have something for you, too."

She rummaged through a box and came up with 2 lagniappes.

"That's nice," said Calvin. "This will look smart on my wall."

"Did I mention we give free consultations?" Sandy asked.

"No," said Calvin. "But as a matter of fact, I've always wanted to put woven wood blinds in Penny Lane."

"A wise idea," said Sandy. "They're very upscale."

"Calvin," said Susan. "Let's go. We still have a few more rounds to make."

"Don't worry," said Sandy. "I'll drop by your place with some samples."

Calvin thanked her, then he and Susan donned their sunglasses and slinked away.

Sandy couldn't have cared less about the condominium proposal or the Merchants' Association's feud with Martin Mall. Her mind was obsessed with loftier thoughts; like the half dozen feelers she'd just put out.

She flipped through the 2 books.

"I'll get to these later," she decided. "Right now, I have a store to unpack."

8

Martin was asleep in his office; adrift in a mall of dreams.

He saw himself as his favorite mannequin, gazing out the window onto Garden Park, dressed in the height of fashion. "This is the good life," he said. He felt proud and content.

All of a sudden, everything went black. A bag had been placed, first over his head, then over his entire body. One of his arms dropped off. Someone put it in his pocket.

Martin was whisked away.

The next thing he knew he was a contestant on a game show. He couldn't understand why anyone would choose a mannequin for a contestant, especially one so ill equipped to applaud. He felt they were taking advantage of him; that he would be made a fool. Still, he listened carefully when the rules were explained.

It seemed simple enough. All he had to do to win was to imagine any grand prize he wanted and it would appear behind either a door or a curtain. His job was to select which.

I should be able to do this, he thought, if I really concentrate. He wished for a father and a mall of his own.

The host, who resembled a bald Calvin Dighby with his plucked eyebrows and superior smirk, told Martin he could have as many chances as he needed, but that most guests succeeded in 2 tries or less, because the prize never changed sides.

"What's it going to be?" he asked. "The curtain or the door?"

Martin wanted to pick the door. The trouble was, he couldn't speak. But everytime the question was repeated the host thought Martin chose the curtain and when the curtain was opened there was always another pair of drapes behind it.

"I'm sorry," said the host. "You'll have to try again."

And again. And again. And again.

The studio audience was getting restless. "Get rid of the idiot," they jeered. "Bring on the next one."

"I'm doing my best," Martin wanted to say. He was beginning to panic. He shivered. He felt some movement in his limbs.

"I hate games!" he shouted. "Stop playing games!"

He woke up.

For a few moments he had trouble remembering where he was. Consciousness finally set in and his dream floated away. The events of the day were seeping back into his mind.

He noticed the manilla envelope and remembered Peaches'

memo. Like all of her notes, it was typed on confidential letterhead and began "it has been brought to my attention..."

Martin read:

CONFIDENTIAL

It has been brought to my attention that this is an exciting time for you. Wonderful. This is an exciting time for all of us. But that's no excuse to go around neglecting your God-given duty. You have a Mall to run! Today's makes 3 missed meetings in a row. What's happening to you? Where's your self-control? And while we're on the subject, let me ask you, who takes the blame for all your little indiscretions? We both know that question has only one reasonable answer and that answer is me. (Your secretary, Peaches del Muhne, in case you've forgotten. You seem to forget everything these days, except for that darn television show of yours.)

Martin Mall, your Shopping Center's calling. Don't you think it's time to answer? If you continue walking around with your head in the clouds, mark my words, it's going to cost you a lot more than my reputation.

My advice: Stay late tonight and catch up on your work. I'm going now. You left me in such a state that the only cure for my nerves is immersion in total untarnished organization. I'll be at home if you need me.

Mend your ways!

The memo was signed with the letter P.

"Nobody understands," he said. "Even Peaches has it in for me. This mall isn't safe anymore. This mall isn't mine."

9

Thanks to the miracle of modular fixtures, designed by Sandy herself, she was able to completely unpack and set up the front half of her store in only a few hours. Now at least it was presentable if anyone else happened by.

Sandy was ready for a diversion. She remembered the two booklets on her shelf. Which will it be, she wondered, the condominium conundrum or a good old fashioned promo kit? She picked up the promo kit. It had a better cover.

Sandy randomly opened the packet to its center section and found a three-dimensional popout of Garden Park. It reminded her of a children's Bible.

She placed the popout on a measuring table and slowly circled around it. The overhead view of the mini-mall was breathtaking... and so lifelike. Simply looking at it gave her vertigo.

She immediately spotted Edgar Portlee in front of his shop. He was a little hard to miss. Next she saw Calvin Dighby and Penny Lane, Susan Carlyle and Prime Jeans, the Wright/Ellis store, the mall's executive offices, 6 kiosks and dozens of other businesses, before she found it; the space allotted to Sheer Curtains.

Sandy bent down to examine it and discovered that it was completely vacant. There wasn't a box or a sample rack in sight. And over the window, on a tiny little sign, were written the words: Coming Soon... A New Concept.

That must have been before we optioned the lease, she thought. (She didn't notice the sign in every single establishment on the vacant second level.)

"Coming soon... a new concept," she repeated. "Sheer Curtains... a new concept." The phrase struck home. Even though she'd never expressed it verbally, that was exactly how she felt prior to opening each store. "That's us in a nutshell," she said. "I know he'd approve..."

Sandy caught herself, just as she was about to mention his name. "I mustn't think of Willy anymore. It's over. I can't keep living in the past."

She pulled up a chair, turned to the first section and plunged into the booklet.

Some people read for information, others to pass the time. Sandy read to forget.

THE BIRTH OF A MALL
by Martin Mall

And there was heaven and there was earth.

And the Lord said, "Not bad for My first try."

And there was day and there was night. And there was winter and there was summer.

And in winter the days were freezing cold. And in summer the days were hot and humid.

And there were deodorants.

And there was air conditioning. And there was heat. And there were big woolly sweaters.

And there were power mowers and televisions and hair dryers and electric can openers.

And there was formica.

Yea, there were all these condiments to be bought and sold and a plethora of places to buy and sell them, but still the people were edgy.

And they complained to each other on a regular basis.

"Why should we have to drive all over town just to go shopping?"

"Why should we have to worry about validated parking?"

"Why do all the stores close before we get home from work?"

Why... why... why...

Until the day they set up a grievance committee and made an appointment to see the Lord.

This is the gist of the proposal they submitted unto Him: "Technology is no Eden. We want everything under one roof!"

"Can't you leave Me alone?" said the Lord. "You're never satisfied." And He started muttering to Himself, "Everything under one roof. They want everything under... one... roof.... Everything under one roof. That's it. That's the answer. It's so simple, I can't believe it."

And He said to the delegation, "Look, you may have come up with something decent for a change. Let Me sleep on it. I'll get back to you tomorrow."

That very evening, the Lord summoned up the finest Architects, Draftspeople, Builders, Engineers, Designers and Optimists (in short, His peer group). And he ran the proposal up the flagpole for them.

And lo and behold, though nary a one served a moment in the military, the Lord's words so inspired them that they saluted in unison and remain at attention until the Lord was forced to say, "at ease."

And the proposal became an idea. And the idea became a concept. And the concept of malls was born.

And the Lord said, "I've got to give credit where credit is due."

And so there was Visa and Mastercharge and American Express.

And the people rejoiced.

In the days that followed, the seeds of many malls began to sprout and blossom in every corner of the land.

There was Cloverdale and Westdale and Southdale and Southwestdale.

And Southwestdale begat Parkdale. Which begat Parkdale Gardens. Which begat the Lincoln Overview Development Corporation. Which begat 5 scores of malls from coast to coast...

Which begat Garden Park.

And Garden Park was a full 5 and 20 years old. And it had led a successful and profitable life.

On the eve of its Grand Reopening and Anniversary Celebrations, let us raise our glasses in a toast to Garden Park: "May your cash never cease to flow..."

HALLELUJAH!

* * *

THE CONFESSIONS OF GARDEN PARK
(as told to Martin Mall)

I was not always a mall.

I was once a famous botanical garden and many, many things before that.

But that was long ago, in the days when people believed that shrubs and greenery had no business taking up profitable downtown space and belonged exclusively in the suburbs.

A lot has changed since then.

Plants and commerce reconciled their differences several years back. I myself, have undergone a number of physical renovations and facelifts. The neighborhood has been redeveloped. Stores come and go.

Yet through it all, I have remained spiritually untouched. True to my original concept, if I do say so myself.

I still welcome customers from 9 to 9, still offer an overabundance of convenient free parking and, most important, still maintain my namesake, a garden in the center of the mall.

You may have seen it. It's hard to miss.

I like to think of it as a monument to days gone by, a tribute to the present and a hope for the future.

Many of the merchants don't agree with that philosophy. More than once they suggested turning it into valuable kiosk space. "It could bring in a helluva revenue," they said.

What do store owners know about aesthetics?

The garden stays where it is.

"An oasis in the middle of a shopping experience; a haven for customers who wish to sit back and enjoy a few moments of peace before moving on to their all-consuming lives." That's what it says on the plaque by the bridge.

There are plenty of benches, a few well placed rocks and a small babbling brook covered with coins.

Naturally the garden is full of plants of all shapes, sizes and denominations; always perfectly arranged and meticulously cared for.

Those of you who've been paying attention will have noticed that my plants never die, never grow wild or unkempt, never speak unless first spoken to.

They're the symbol of my unrelenting quest for survival. You can hardly tell they're plastic.

I was here. I am here. I will always be here.
>   I've been many things at many times
>   buildings large and small,
>   a bridge of steel, a catacomb...
>   Today I am a mall.

CHEERS!

* * *

Sandy was fascinated by the promo kit, but she was having trouble keeping her eyes open. She'd had a long, hard day in an unfamiliar environment. That was always exhausting for her. So rather than pressing on, she resigned herself to the inevitable and fell into a much needed sleep.

10

Every night at 11:30, Martin Mall felt a second urge to browse. He'd leave his office, take the stairway down to the main level and enter the empty mall.

There, he'd don a different personality. He might be a retail baron — owner of a multi-disciplinary chain of stores, surveying his empire — trying to get a jump on the competition. "Now there's a window to be proud of," he would say. "I must find out who's responsible and give them a 50¢ raise."

He could be a sales clerk intent on spending the night, just to find out if mannequins really have sex after closing. And if so, what is their proclivity. "Unbelievable," he'd exclaim, "I just witnessed the birth of Barbie... or Ken."

Sometimes he'd become the Lord High of Malls, the Chief Executive Officer of the Lincoln Overview Development Corporation or CEO of LODC. Then he'd strut down the corridors regally, brimming with pride from his perfectly-ordered world. "This calls for a tribute," he'd say, and begin a recitation of Desiderata.

There was only one character Martin never attempted to be. He never impersonated a customer.

Walking in Garden Park after the stores had closed was a mind-expanding experience for Martin. A man and his mall. There was no commotion, no pressure, no noise.

Nothing.

Except the muzak.

Martin believed that muzak wasn't something you could turn on and off at will. It was the lifeblood of the mall.

"Without its muzak," he always said, "Garden Park wouldn't be Garden Park. And a mall without an identity is worse than no mall at all."

So the muzak played and so did Martin. And just before he'd call it a day, he'd revert back to himself, wander from shop to shop, peer in windows and rattle the doors. He didn't care that Center Security performed the identical task. He couldn't rest until he put his mall to bed.

When he came to Sheer Curtains, Martin noticed that the lights were still on. Disappointed, he made a note to have Peaches send Sandy his recent report on conservation and the retail establishment.

He looked inside once again and was genuinely taken aback. Her place was all neat and tidy; completely set up. Who would have guessed that she'd been there less than 24 hours.

Martin was faced with a dilemma. He couldn't decide whether to admire Sandy or not. "She's a woman of contradictions," he said.

He was about to move on, but he remembered he had to check her door. Someday I've got to break this habit, he thought. In all his years as a watchdog, he never found a store unlocked.

He gave the handle a good, solid shove and was surprised to find himself inside the newly arranged outlet. At first he thought it was deserted. Then he saw her, slumped down behind a row of samples.

"Sandy," he called, "Are you alright?"

Sandy didn't answer. She was flying in that delirious state between waking and slumber. Hearing her name carried her deeper into her reverie.

Sandy was a delegate at a protozoa convention. She and hundreds of other amoeba and parameciums were in a workshop discussing mitosis and the expansion of the single cell. Sandy kept looking behind her. She sensed she was being observed. Even though she couldn't perceive the boundaries, she knew she was on a slide in some laboratory being scrutinized for her attitude and performance. She was on her best behavior. She made an extra effort to participate. "Mitosis," she said, "is second nature to me. I've been practising it for years. And the reason I'm so successful? I won't let my progeny forget I'm the boss."

"Bravo," said a voice that was coming from another planet. Sandy held her cillia as still as possible, waiting for her moment of redemption.

"Willy," she mumbled. "It's him. I knew it. I've got to play it cool. I can't risk losing him again. And she said, in a slightly more audible tone of voice, "Over here. How are you? I'm doing fine."

"I'm glad," said Martin. "I was a little worried. But now that I see you're OK, there's something I have to tell you."

"I hope it's a secret."

"Not quite," he replied. "More like old fashioned common sense."

"Whatever it is," she said, "it's sweet of you to share it."

"Thanks for being so receptive." He cleared his throat. "Well, here goes... I don't care what your excuse is, you should never leave..."

"Oh Willy, Willy," she interrupted. "You always know what to say. I'll never, ever leave you. I promise I won't. I've missed you so much. I didn't even get a chance to say goodbye. From now on, things will be different. Your wish is my command. I'll follow you anywhere."

She ran directly into Martin's arms.

"Willy," she cried, "I love you."

"I'm sorry," said Martin, "I didn't realize you were expecting a guest. I was just checking the mall and I noticed your door was unlocked. I wanted to warn you... to be careful. I didn't mean to intrude. Please, forgive me."

He started backing away from Sandy and inching out of the store.

"It's you," said Sandy. "I'm so embarrassed. I'm really not like this. I hope you'll accept my apologies."

"No harm done," said Martin. He was too shy to ask her about Willy.

"I suppose this is a coincidence," she said, trying to change the subject.

"What is?"

"I was just reading your book. The Merchants' Association gave it to me this afternoon."

"That's strange," said Martin. "Nothing I do seems to please them. They told me they hated it."

"I can't understand that," she said. "The whole thing captivated me."

"Is that why you fell asleep?"

"Not fair," she replied. "You should learn to accept a compliment graciously."

"You're right," said Martin. "Thank you. It's just that lately I've had to deal with a lot of negativity and I guess I'm trying to protect myself."

"No need to explain," she said. "Did you conceive the entire package?"

"Most of it."

"You're very talented. I envy you."

"That's silly," he said. "I'm sure you do many things that I couldn't possibly compete with. Like selling drapes, for example."

"You're right," she said. Sandy was never one for false modesty.

"But one thing I'm positive I know better than you," Martin continued, "is Garden Park. What I mean to say is, if you're not too tired, maybe I could show you around the mall right now. Help get you oriented. That is, if you really don't have a prior commitment."

"That's a wonderful idea," said Sandy. She pointed to the pop-out on the table. "Although I feel like I've already been there."

I knew it, he thought, it does work. Wait till that Merchants' Association hears about this.

Martin's sagging self-confidence was beginning to feel erect.

11

"There's a lot of scaffolding," said Martin, referring to the renovations. "I'm sorry. Looks like you can see the mall better from the popout. Right now, anyway, it's a more accurate picture."

They decided to skip the tour and Martin led Sandy directly to the garden. Or, as he preferred to call it (complete with French accent), the mall's "pièce de résistance." She grasped the meaning of the epithet as soon as they arrived.

Seeing the garden at such close proximity and without anyone around, was a truly profound experience for Sandy. It stripped away all of her protective defenses and made her both humble and shy. Yet at the same time, it excited her.

"This is even more breathtaking than I imagined," she said. "It's a paradise."

"I agree," Martin replied.

He handed Sandy a coin and told her that if she threw it into the brook all her wishes would come true. She closed her eyes and wished for a world with more windows.

Martin seized the opportunity and guided her to his favorite bench.

"If you sit perfectly still," he said, "you can almost hear the echo of sales — past, present and future."

"You're so sensitive."

"Sandy, if I confide in you, will you promise not to spread it around?"

"Word of honor," she said.

"I have visions," said Martin.

"I believe it," Sandy replied.

"Remember the mall that caved in last year?"

"Vaguely."

"I saw it happen."

"You were there?"

"Not exactly."

"Then how..."

"It came to me while I was lying in bed," he said. "The image of a quiet, empty mall, deserted, except for three little pigs, who were happily playing inside. Suddenly, this big, black Cadillac pulled up and a very mean wolf got out. He said he didn't care what time it was, he wanted to do his shopping and no one could stop him. The pigs tried to say that everything was closed and that he'd have to come back tomorrow. He accused them of lying, huffed and puffed and blew the mall down. I woke up in a cold sweat. It was awful."

"I'll bet," she replied.

"The next morning when I turned on the radio," Martin continued, "I heard about this disaster. After that, I couldn't eat bacon for months."

"That's amazing," she said. "Do you get these visions often?"

"Not too often. Once in a while. But when they happen, I take them seriously."

Sandy could relate to that.

"I may have had one tonight," Martin said.

"No kidding. What was it about?"

"I'm not sure. I remember a game show and a studio audience. And Calvin Dighby, without any hair... And for whatever reason I kept picking these curtains."

"Do you think that had something to do with me?" she asked.

"I doubt it," he said. "It's too literal. Still, anything is possible..."

Martin became introspective. He was trying to reconstruct his dream. He almost succeeded, when Sandy began to feel very alone and panicked. The sound of her voice abruptly brought him back to his senses.

"What's that aroma?" she asked.

Martin inhaled. "Nostalgia," he replied.

"Pardon me?"

He explained to her that the fragrance she was enjoying was 1968.

"A unique blend of incense, Love Lemmon perfume and brand new tie-dyed T-shirts. And if you listen closely, you'll notice that the muzak is only playing Donovan tunes."

Sandy perked up her ears. "Well what do you know."

"Here at Garden Park, we believe that sound and smell are an integral part of the shopping experience. So we contracted nostalgia specialists to recreate the past. They designed a total package for us that takes our customers back to less pressured economic times. As soon as they walk through our doors, they forget about their petty problems. Being here rejuvenates them. And, speaking demographically, a rejuvenated customer is a healthier spender."

"C'mon, level with me. Does this system of yours really increase sales?"

"We've got the figures to prove it."

"And figures don't lie," she mumbled. That was one of her father's primary philosophies.

Sandy realized her throat was dry, there were butterflies in her stomach and her head was swimming. "That's odd," she said. "I feel like I'm in love."

They stared at each other then abruptly turned away. "It's part of the effect," he replied.

"No kidding. You mean you feel the same?"

"Yes... and No." He was thinking about the young girl from the Republic Cigar Kiosk. "I'm used to it," he added.

"This is one strange mall. Seymour will be impressed."

"Who?"

"Seymour. Seymour Black. He's my boss."

Martin registered disappointment. "I thought your father owned Sheer Curtains. At lunch Edgar said..."

"Edgar couldn't have known," she replied. "It hasn't made the trades. About 4 weeks ago, we were bought out by Seymour Black and Isaiah Productions."

"Whatever for?" he asked.

"They wanted to diversify."

"That's funny," Martin said. "I spoke to Seymour Black this afternoon and for the life of me I couldn't figure out who he was. Now it all makes sense. Seymour Black, the film producer."

"And Chairman of the Board of Sheer Curtains Inc.," she quickly added.

"He told me he wanted to meet me; that the two of us would have a lot in common."

"Just like you," she said, "he's very conceptual."

"Yes, but does he follow through?"

"I'm afraid he does," Sandy replied and she sadly lamented the fact that she was no longer an independent. "In some ways you resemble each other. I wonder if you're related."

"Even if we were," said Martin, "it wouldn't get you a better deal on the lease."

On their way back to Sheer Curtains, Sandy and Martin were silent.

"I'd invite you in," she said, "except I have nothing to serve. On the other hand, we could always go back to your office. I'd love to measure your windows."

"At this hour?"

"A good salesperson," she replied, "never carries a watch."

12

Sandy put her sample bag on Martin's desk. She was relieved to find that everything in his office looked as drab and dull as earlier that afternoon.

Martin offered her a coffee.

"Later," she said. She was too excited to drink.

"I suppose," said Martin, "that you've already picked the style and color and all you want me to do is OK it."

Sandy's bubble burst. He's wrong, she thought. I haven't chosen it, yet.

"You know, Martin," she said, "you have a convoluted view of salespeople. You completely misunderstand our role in the universe of retail consumption. The decisions are yours. We are advisors. We're here to help. For your benefit. We don't subvert your brains. We don't select what you will or won't buy. We don't start wars..."

"Wait a minute," Martin interrupted defensively, "I never said you did."

"Let me finish!" Sandy shot back. "To tell you the truth, I'm surprised at you. Frankly I expected more from a man of your background and taste. Now if you'll excuse me, I'd best be on my way."

"Please," said Martin. "I had no idea I was offending you. I just wanted..."

"You didn't offend me," Sandy replied. "I was just disappointed, that's all. Good-bye."

"Sandy, wait, I..."

"I'll tell you something, Martin. My life would be pretty dull if all I ever did was practise subliminal customer manipulation. I'd only need 1 sample."

She laughed and motioned to her shop-at-home suitcase. "What would be the point? To me, the beauty of selling is the spontaneity. There's always something new, every time. But really, I've overstayed my welcome."

"Sandy, please. I beg you, don't go. I mean at least not before you give me a quick estimate. I mean, you came all the way up here with your samples and everything. You've got to believe me. I'm sorry I questioned your motives. It's just that..."

She was warming up to him again.

"...It's just that, I didn't know how to handle it. I was nervous.

You see, this is the first time. I've never ordered a pair of drapes before."

"You're kidding me, aren't you?" Sandy was shocked. She'd never met anyone who hadn't purchased at least one set of drapes.

"I'm dead serious," he replied. "So please stay. Without you, I wouldn't know where to begin."

"Well," Sandy said, "Maybe I will reconsider."

"I hope so."

"Why don't we start with the fabric?" she asked as she hoisted the sample book onto his desk.

"So soon? Do you honestly think I'm ready?"

"Don't worry," Sandy reassured. "I'll be gentle." She winked at Martin. He averted his eyes and began to blush.

This is better than I planned, she thought. She opened a sample book and began flipping through it, half talking to Martin, half to herself.

"This one's nice. This one's not bad. No... No... Wrong color. This is sort of like the first one. You're not thrilled with it, are you? I can tell. You know, it's amazing how a single company can put out so much junk and still come out with a decent line every now and then. But I guess that's showbiz. So, where were we? Oh yes... dull, mediocre, uninteresting...Wait a minute. What do you think of this? It certainly stands out, doesn't it? Why don't we hold it up to your window — just to get an idea of what it looks like in here. Not bad. Not bad at all. It definitely goes with your color scheme. It even brings out that little fleck in your carpet and the frames on your awards. I'll tell you, this material complements everything in your office. I like it a lot. But there's no sense jumping the gun. Let's put it aside and have a quick look at the rest. Who knows? Maybe we can come up with something we like even better?"

"From "I" to "we" in under 5 minutes. There was no doubt about it, Sandy had what it took and she knew how to use it.

They glanced through the remaining samples, repeating the procedure and finally managed to narrow the choices down to the 2 fabrics Sandy had pre-selected in advance.

"So," she said, "we've gone this far. Think you can handle the rest?"

Martin nodded sheepishly.

"Then I guess we're ready for the foreplay."

"I beg your pardon," he said half swallowing his words. "Sandy... Ms. Rodd... I hardly know you..."

"Calm down. I wasn't referring to what you think I was referring to. I'm not *that* kind of person..."

"So what kind are you?"

"I'm a salesperson," she said, quoting her mentor. "And a salesperson's got to sell."

Martin was getting another headache. He began to regret that he'd ever run into Sandy; that he'd bothered to invite her back to his office. A drapery estimate, he thought. What a flimsy excuse. And to make matters worse, he wasn't even sure if he wanted a new set of curtains. All this trouble for nothing. Why didn't Sandy leave when she threatened to earlier? Why is life so complicated? Why does everything seem to get out of hand?

"Martin... Martin, are you OK?" Sandy asked. "I brought you a glass of water. You looked kind of pale."

"Thank you," said Martin. "I'm fine. I just went away for a moment. I guess I've been working too hard."

"I know we've been through this before, but I could come back tomorrow. Or not at all. Whichever you prefer."

"That won't be necessary," he replied. "I'm alright, really. So please, let's continue."

"What I was trying to tell you earlier," Sandy said, "has nothing to do with you and me. It has to do with the logistics of the sale, getting all the details out of the way. Then we're free to concentrate all our energy on the creative requirements of the room."

"And what details might these be?" Martin asked skeptically.

"You know," said Sandy, "measuring the windows, choosing a track, picking the right type of pleat... That kind of stuff. Shall we get on with it?"

"If anyone would have told me that buying drapes was such an intricate procedure, I would never have believed them. Oh, what the hell. We've gone this far. We might as well go all the way."

"Great," said Sandy. "I'm glad you've come around. Now, if you could just grab the other end of this steel tape and hold it. No, that's too tight. There, you've got it. Perfect. I'm telling you, you'll be a drapery salesperson yet."

Sandy measured and re-measured the windows, marking the numbers down first on a scrap piece of paper and then transferring them to a small looseleaf notebook.

"What is that?" he asked.

"Some people collect stamps," she replied, "I happen to prefer window measurements."

"You're lucky. At least your hobby's work related."

"If you don't mind," she said, "I have to ask you a few questions about your preferences."

"My..."

"For drapery hardware," she continued. "Please don't take this personally. It's all in the line of duty."

"I understand," he said, "Fire away."

Martin stood up fairly well to Sandy's interrogation, considering that drapery hardware was not one of his strong suits. Before long, the preliminaries were over and all that stood between Sandy and another successful sale was the physical act itself.

Easy as pie, she thought. She knew she had Martin in the palm of her hand. She'd won him over with her definition of foreplay.

"Excuse me," he said, "I'm not sure if this is part of my domain, but you haven't mentioned vertical blinds. And I know for a fact that a lot of office administrators swear by them."

Sandy made a face. She was an old-fashioned type, who preferred the calm elegance of drapes to the harsh modernism of verticals.

"That's precisely the reason I don't recommend them," she said. "They're too popular with the layman. When I finish with a room, I want it to have that little extra magic. I won't settle for anything less than a one of a kind. Besides, I just don't happen to see verticals as part of your decorating concept."

"Sandy Rodd," said Martin, "I like your style."

Sandy didn't respond. The time was right, she felt, to take the leap. She didn't want to postpone the moment of ecstasy any longer.

She started breathing heavily, hyperventilating, almost. This alarmed Martin. He asked her if he should call a doctor.

Between gasps, Sandy told him not to worry. She was just getting into the zen of the estimate.

Meanwhile, Sandy was overcome by the effects of her meditation. Every muscle in her body had loosened and relaxed. Her mind was being elevated to a loftier plane where banalities and the trivial no longer mattered. The sale. That was most important. The sale. The sale. All she could think about was the sale.

"Let's see," she mumbled to Martin, "18 feet, doubled... no tripled... that's 4 carry 1... 14 panels times 3½ yards is..."

Sandy swooned. Just a few more minutes and she would be

ready to give herself to the sale, fully and without hesitation. She longed for that moment to draw nearer, prayed for it in her soul.

And then it happened. Slowly, but with an increasing intensity and strength.

"My god," said Sandy, "It *is* beautiful."

Suddenly her heart was palpitating. Her arms were flailing about in a frenzied motion. Sandy was unable to control the sounds; the little yelps of joy that came pouring from her mouth.

She was drowning in the pleasure of the estimate. But oh, she thought, what a way to go!

Sandy was almost there. Her body was undulating; her blood was rushing through her veins. Faster, faster, faster. She was exploding. She experienced a wave of total creative control.

"90 yards," she shouted, "Triple fullness! Triple fullness! Triple fullness!!!"

Sandy was perspiring. She tried to catch her breath. Her lips were moving ever so slightly and only the remnants of sounds were seeping through. Her eyes sparkled. The beginning of a smile appeared on her face.

"Would you like to place the order now?" she heard herself say.

Martin was awestruck. He wasn't sure whether to answer or applaud. "Of course... Sure... Why not... Where do I sign..." was all he could muster. "Hey, you forgot something," he added. "We haven't decided what fabric I'm taking."

Sandy had quick reflexes. "It doesn't matter," she said, puffing. "They're both the same price. You can sleep on it and call me in the morning."

When all the paper work had been done and the order was signed and sealed, they sat down and Martin poured them each a coffee. Sandy was still puffing. She wanted a cigarette. She asked Martin if he had one.

"I don't smoke," he said.

Sandy replied that she didn't either. She used to, she said, but she had to give it up.

"I used to light a cigarette every time I made a sale — until I noticed I was chain smoking." She shrugged. "Oh well, I guess it's pretty late. Can I give you a ride home?"

"No thanks," Martin said, "This is where I live."

Sandy looked around the shabby office and thought of all her stores, in all the malls, and all the hours she spent there.

"I know what you mean, Martin. I know exactly what you mean."

PHASE II

13
OBITUARY

The world mourns Seymour Black, self-styled lawyer, rabbi, investor, film producer, retail magnate and all-round genius — a man who rose from relative obscurity (a 3-bedroom bungalow in the suburbs) to reach the very middle of our society. That is to say its heart.

Time in a conventional sense did not exist for Seymour Black. Careers intended as lifelong pursuits were but drops in the bottom of his bucket. A year... a decade... a day... They seldom lasted.

Then he passed through them.
   Then he passed over them.
      Then he passed away.

Suddenly!

And with a few regrets....

Seymour was a perfectionist. He was noted for many accomplishments. A complete and authorized biography is available from his holding company, Isaiah Productions (please include a S.A.S.E.). It would be an injustice to list his deeds here.

If he had one flaw — and there were those who claimed he had many — if there was a single deficiency that plagued him throughout his life, it was neither his obsessive nature, nor his volatile attention span. Neither his snap judgements, nor his ego out of control. Seymour's nemesis was his success. It pursued him with a vengeance. It sneaked up on him from behind and held a knife to his throat. No matter how many times he turned his back on it, everything he touched turned to gold (especially his credit cards).

But Seymour wasn't seeking gold. He didn't covet filthy lucre. (He did enjoy them, mind you.) No. His ambitions were on a loftier plane.

Seymour craved immortality. "A development named everlasting," was how he decribed it. More than life after death, he was shooting for life after life.

Whenever he distinguished himself — lawyer, rabbi, investor, producer, retail magnate (he had CEO's coming out of his ears) — he did so with one end in mind. He wasn't out for the glory, although there was plenty to go around. He didn't lust after power. He had power to spare. Eternity was his biway. Too bad he got off at the wrong exit.

All he achieved, the accolades, the cash flow, the tremendous press, couldn't help him realize his dream. This epitome of success failed at the one thing he desired most. The irony being, he'll never know he didn't make it. Or perhaps that's his solace.

His final request was that the words to "Elusive Butterfly," a song he never tired of hearing, be emblazoned on his mausoleum.

Seymour Black is survived by those who had the pleasure and those who didn't.

Public reception and tribute following the funeral. Admission free. Reservations required.

* * *

Seymour Black pressed the print command button on his user-ambivalent computer. He waited a moment for the clicking to stop, then removed the paper and scrutinized his work.

A mood obituary, he thought. He was trying something different. Theme oriented as opposed to statistical. "It's objective," he said, "yet I come across well. Destiny and pathos. A good combination."

Seymour Black revised his obituary every 3 or so months. It was a game he played, a way of testing his immortality. Each time he survived another obituary, he felt he was outliving himself and therefore getting closer to his ultimate goal. And in a purely practical sense this ritual doubled as his insurance policy — just in case he failed (which he doubted). If (and he hated to even think this) he should die suddenly, there was no point trusting the arrangements to chance. He decided long ago that he would plan for every contingency. Seymour was impulsive, but never one to improvise. In addition to his death release and notarized will, he would leave behind such a complex set of directives that the full effect of his absence would not be felt for at least 10 years.

"Cheryl," he called into the intercom. "Could you please step into my office. I have something for you to xerox."

"Which office?" she asked. He didn't hear her mumble, "Why don't you bring it here yourself?"

"Which do you think," he said. "The Seymour office. It's Monday morning. And hurry please. I'm getting tense."

It took Cheryl almost 10 minutes to reach Seymour Black. He was in the innermost of his inner sanctums and to get there she had to pass through 5 distinct rooms interconnected by 5 separate corridors. There was no short cut.

Seymour kept a fully furnished and operational office for each of his undertakings. So in order to see him, you literally had to make your way through the major facets of his adult life. A chronological tour. Seymour wanted people to empathize with the changes and turmoil that brought him to his present state. Every room Cheryl entered was left just as it was when Seymour was centered there. The rabbi's study, with its dark wood, leather chairs, bookshelves and robes, had an air of wisdom to it. The producer's quarters were glitzy and spacious and had plenty of track lighting. Signed movie posters hung symmetrically on the walls.

The offices maintained their original phone numbers and housed most of their old files and correspondence. The only similarity between them were the walls, which were all painted grey. "That's my only stipulation," Seymour would say to the decorator he hired everytime he acquired a new interest, "that and the fact that my private sanctuary has to be as far back as possible from public access." Capitalism was causing Seymour Black to retreat deeper into himself.

Cheryl breezed in. "What took you so long?" he asked. "I told you I was in a rush."

"The phone rang in your production suite. I had to get it."

"Who was it?"

"Some young director," she replied. "He said he has a great idea for the definitive airport film."

"Didn't he hear I stopped making airport pictures? They're out. Finished. Passé... And anyway, you're not supposed to talk movies in here. This is my personal space. Reserved for Seymour, the human being... Period. Do you understand?"

Cheryl nodded. She looked around the sparse, but well-designed room. There was virtually no color to it. The desk, wall unit, chairs, couch, even the computer were all done in shades of grey. It reminded Cheryl of "The Outer Limits." The effect boggled her mind.

It reminded Seymour that without immortality everything was a grey zone; there were no absolutes. It also reminded him of the grey matter in his brain, which was working overtime to propel him to forever.

"Will there be anything else?" Cheryl asked.

"Yes," he said. "I need 50 of these. Send them out pronto to the regular list and file the original in the safe. My new obituary," he added.

"What's wrong with the old one?" she mumbled as she left.

Seymour stared at his terminal (life) for a full 2 minutes prior to shutting it down. He moved to his Sheer Curtains office, which, being his latest acquisition, was situated next door to his inner sanctum.

The Sheer Curtains project depressed him a little. It was so different from anything he had ever done. He wondered if he'd overstepped his bounds. He was used to dealing in ideas, concepts, themes. He didn't know what to make of a tangible product.

But there they were. Racks of neatly arranged samples. And Seymour was systematically learning them by touch. Even though he had no intention of doing any selling, his personality made it essential that he discover as much as possible about whatever it was that involved him.

Three weeks earlier, he couldn't tell the difference between a dye lot or a pleat. Now he marvelled at the subtleties that defined each fabric. The philosophy behind the choice of verticals or venetians. The science of retail.

How did he get himself into this one? His life had been moving smoothly. Too smoothly, possibly. He was a producer who enjoyed his work. He'd just completed negotiations for a 12-part mini-series. He was content. He moved easily from career to career, taking care of business like Bachman Turner Overdrive. He was finally settling into a routine.

And this petrified him.

A routine... Stability...

He was starting to take root. He felt it. Soon he would flower and die. And immortality would fade from his soul.

So why wait, Seymour reasoned. He contemplated suicide. A fatal injection of peanut oil, a substance he was violently allergic to. He purchased a small jar of the lethal compound and a diabetic's syringe. The blatant rebelliousness of buying his death tools so openly (he asked a clerk to recommend the nuttiest brand) — made him giddy with excitement. He was high as a kite.

He played out his demise: blotchy hives, swollen eyes, itchy throat, lungs barely able to process oxygen, heart thumping erratic-ally.... The scene was so vivid that it brought on a mild allergic reaction. Without thinking, Seymour swallowed 3 antihistamines and fell into a hypnotic sleep.

He imagined himself in a darkened room. Every wall was covered with drapes. Some type of brocade, he sensed it. The pitch blackness made it impossible for him to know whether his eyes were open or closed.

He panicked.

"I didn't mean to kill myself," he screamed. "Please God, or whoever you are, give me another chance!"

Suddenly one of the curtains parted. Just like the Red Sea. Seymour glimpsed a bliss he never dreamed existed. This must be the everlasting, he thought. And he shouted, "Thank you. I appreciate it..."

"It's amazing," he mused, "curtains — I'm sorry I never noticed — you are the eyes of the world..."

"If everyone," he went on, "could open their eyes, I mean their curtains, at precisely the same moment, the sheer effect of all the light, would be instant immortality. Why didn't I see it before?"

He awoke from his revelation motivated and refreshed. But not without a proper perspective. Seymour realized getting all those drapes to open simultaneously might be a difficult task. Nevertheless, he was determined to accomplish it.

Soon he was on the phone. Before the hour was out, he summoned his staff. Before the day was out, he had a list of half a dozen viable drapery chains. Before the week was out, he purchased Sheer Curtains, lock, stock and remnant barrel.

Seymour experienced a wave of elation.

Unfortunately, buying Sheer Curtains did not give him the answer he was seeking. Still he didn't lose his optimism. And that was a good sign.

"The secrets of the universe," he said, "must dwell deep within the house of retail."

Seymour prayed for the key to unlock them. He was tired. He'd journeyed a long way; from law to religion, to investments, to filmmaking, to customer service. Now enveloped in a luke-warm glow. Seymour felt the promised land was almost in his grasp.

14

The night before Sheer Curtains' grand opening, Sandy Rodd slept in the store. Actually, she didn't sleep as much as attend to the myriad of details that had to be taken care of before the next day: moving a display here, a fixture there, memorizing the exact location of each sample and on and on and on...

She didn't mind, though. She told herself it was the price of perfection.

When she opened her eyes in the morning, she liked what she saw. But this is no time for vanity, she thought.

She hurried over to her hotel for a quick shower and breakfast and practised drapery estimates as she ate.

When she returned, she was surprised to find the lights already switched on.

"Hello Sandy," said a voice. "You're looking pretty chipper, today."

"Hello?... Oh, hello Seymour," she replied flatly. "I should've known it would be you. When did you arrive?"

"A little over an hour ago," he said.

"So what do you think of the store?"

"A work of art," he answered. "I like the new touches. You've really outdone yourself."

"Thank you," said Sandy.

There was a loud clinking of keys as the door to Sheer Curtains was relocked, pushed to no avail, and finally reopened. Harry Rodd grunted as he entered, sliding the door closed behind him.

"Anybody home?" he asked. "Sandy, I've brought the... My god, don't tell me I'm the last one in... So what are we waiting for? Let's get started."

Sandy rolled her eyes. "Daddy, relax," she said. "You just got here. And besides, you didn't even ask me how I am."

"I'm sorry," said Harry, "I just feel a little guilty. Like I'm neglecting my duty. You know there was a time when I'd beat everyone into the store by over an hour. I must be getting old."

Seymour didn't argue.

"So that's how you feel," Harry said. "Well for your information, Mr. ex-Talmudic scholar, I happen to be a very young 59. And just because you're 3 years my junior, don't think you're in that much better shape than me, either."

"I didn't think anything, Harry," Seymour replied, "except that you should stop kvetching. We have a store to run."

Harry turned beet red. The one thing he hated more than Seymour's lucky business sense was Seymour's rabbinical advice. He's got a lot of nerve, thought Harry. There's a world of difference between a man of cloth and a man of the cloth. Seymour just can't get that through his thick skull.

Harry felt it was a conflict of interest for Seymour to be in the drapery business. Harry was a very religious man.

"You'll never guess who I ran into, Daddy," Sand said. "Edgar Portlee."

"Edgar Portlee," Harry replied, "that crook! Did he tell you we were partners? The louse still owes me $200."

"That's not a lot of money," Sandy said. "Don't you think you should let bygones be bygones?"

"I could care less about the money," Harry said.

"That's a new one," Seymour interjected. "When did you pick up this philosophy?"

"It's the principle of the thing," Harry continued. "All Eddie had to do was call or something. When you're in business together, you should act like a professional."

"I hate to interrupt this fascinating discourse," Seymour said, "but it is almost 9:30 and we should be opening the sliding doors."

Harry was turning colors again. "Stop telling me how to run my shop... Excuse me, our shop. I know perfectly well when we have to open. I've being doing it for over 30 years now and without your help, thank you very much. I think I'm still capable of deciding when it's time to let people in." He looked at his watch. "Sandy, slide open the front door. And while you're at it, could you please pass me a nitro."

Sheer Curtains grand opening was slightly less momentous than either Sandy, Harry or Seymour had anticipated. Only 3 customers were waiting at the gate. Two were interested in dress fabrics, the third in bathroom accessories. Sandy was getting tense. She was hungry for a good drapery order.

"Well Sandy," said Seymour, "where are all the customers you promised?"

"They'll be here."

"You don't think maybe we've jumped the gun," he said. "Perhaps we should have waited a couple of weeks and piggybacked on the shopping center's Grand Reopening celebrations."

"Sometimes it's better to start quietly," she replied, "and build up a good word of mouth."

"If you'll pardon the analogy, in the film business if a sequel to a hit doesn't catch fire in the first few days, you may as well bury it. Do you follow me?"

"What are you saying, Seymour?" Sandy asked. "Do you want me to resign?"

"Don't be so touchy. I'm just trying to learn the business. I always explore every possibility."

15

Martin Mall learned early, never to judge a store by the number of customers present for its inauguration. Unlike Seymour, he knew retail was a living entity. You had to stand back and let it grow.

"It looks like you're off to a rousing start," he said without a trace of irony in his voice. "I thought I'd drop by to wish you the best and also to check on my drapery order."

"Hello Martin," Sandy said. "Thanks for coming. Let me introduce you to my father and Seymour. Seymour, Dad, this is Martin Mall, Manager and Chief Conceptualizer of Garden Park."

"A pleasure," said Harry.

"The pleasure is mine," Martin replied. He turned to Seymour and extended his hand. "I've been anticipating our meeting all week."

Seymour smiled and gave Martin his card. Martin stared at it for a moment. The 3-D lettering seemed to jump from the paper: "Seymour Black; Isaiah Productions; Our pictures always make a profit."

"This isn't the first time we've met," said Seymour.

Martin was visibly embarrassed. He usually had an excellent memory for names and faces.

"I'm sorry," he confessed, "I don't remember..."

"No matter, it was a long time ago. And it's definitely not the reason I wanted to see you. I have a business proposition to discuss."

"It must be some deal," Martin said, "considering how hard you tried to reach me. What are you planning to do? Buy the mall?"

"I hadn't thought of that," Seymour replied. "But it's not a bad idea. Maybe we should get together privately for lunch?"

"That depends on who's picking up the tab."

"I like a man who doesn't mince words," Seymour said. "Today it's my treat."

"Then what are we waiting for?" Martin said. "It was very nice meeting you Mr. Rodd. I'm sure we'll be seeing each other soon. Oh, I almost forgot, Edgar Portlee wanted me to give you something."

He handed Harry an envelope. Harry grumbled as he tore it open. "What is this... Well, what do you know? $250. Eddie, that old son-of-a-gun. He remembered."

Edgar was waiting for Harry's reaction. He rushed in the minute he saw him holding the cash.

"Harry, how've you been?" asked Edgar.

"Eddie, you old snake. You haven't change a bit. It looks like retail really agrees with you."

"You too, Harry. What can I tell you? How long has it been?"

"Too long," said Harry. "And by the way, there was no need to add the interest."

"Harry, keep the change. You know, I'm really sorry about the dough. I kept meaning to send it to you. I just never got around to it. Every year that went by made me feel worse. But I got busy. One store here... Another there... An ulcer... I lost track of time. So when your lovely daughter Sandy told me you were coming to town, I made up my mind, enough is enough. 27 years without your best friend and the best darn business partner you've ever had is too long. Do you think we could pick up where we left off?"

"Eddie," said Harry, "I'm willing if you are."

Suddenly the two men were hugging.

"Is this good for business?" Seymour asked.

"Seymour, come here," Harry said. "I'd like you to meet Edgar Portlee, my oldest and dearest friend."

"We both graduated from the school of hard knocks," Edgar said.

"Then this must be your class reunion," said Seymour. "I hope you'll forgive me if I don't stick around for the festivities. I've never been much of an alumnus myself. Shall we, Martin?"

"Ready when you are," he said. "Bye Sandy. See you later, everyone."

"Make them count," said Seymour, referring to the customers.

"Who's he?" Edgar said.

"Don't ask," Harry replied. "Eddie, I can see we need to catch up. Why don't we retire to the executive lounge and talk awhile? Sandy, we'll be in the stockroom. Can you manage alright without me?"

Sandy didn't respond. She was too busy wooing a customer.

"That'll be $740 plus tax," she said to her unsuspecting prey. "Would you like to place the order now?"

16

At Seymour's insistence and against Martin's better judgement, the two men left Garden Park to lunch at Bob and Jerry's, a western-style steak house. The restaurant looked like a 50s motel that had all its windows removed. A circular overhang by the front door protected its patrons from snow, rain or shine. Inside everything was dark and sleek, the color of charbroiled beef. Except for the chairs which were blood-red vinyl.

Martin felt uncomfortable there. He was surrounded by the enemy: doctors, lawyers, accountants, professionals... People who worked in the suburbs, but shopped downtown. People who scorned the very idea of malls. They had lifestyles to maintain. And they made sure everyone knew it. Martin heard snippets of derogatory remarks aimed at the mall from several corners of the room. This blatant disregard for all he held dear made him feel self-conscious and squirm in his seat.

Martin's state of mind wasn't helped by the fact that he didn't get along with the restaurant's owners. He resented any business that was able to make a go of things outside the context of his mall. He felt its very existence was a personal affront to his managerial prowess.

And that was only the tip of the iceberg. Martin disliked Bob and Jerry for other reasons, too. Like the time they outbid Garden Park for the location of the celebrity telethon. Or when Martin extended his hospitality and offered them a prime location.

"What do we need your place for?" Jerry asked. "We're right across the ravine so we draw on your traffic."

"It's the best of both worlds," Bob added. "We have plenty of free parking plus we own our own land. Maybe you should consider working for us."

Their words still stung.

When Bob and Jerry came over to greet Seymour, a friend-from-the-old-days, Martin gave them the cold shoulder.

"You know these guys, don't you?" Seymour asked.

"We've met," Martin replied.

Bob and Jerry stayed for a minute. Then the tuxedoed-duo excused themselves and sauntered off to another table. It seemed like everyone in the restaurant was a friend-from-the-old-days.

"Great guys," said Seymour. "A class act. They built this place up from a greasy spoon. Hard to believe, isn't it? I used to spend a lot of time here. They had a kosher kitchen that specialized in catered affairs. Nothing compared with one of their charbroiled do's. They got me through many a receiving line... So. Decided what you're having for lunch?"

Martin shrugged. Lunch? How could he think about lunch? All he wanted to do was rush back to his office. Martin was a displaced personality outside Garden Park.

"I'm not very hungry," he told Seymour. "And besides, I have a feeling I'm needed back at the center."

"You have a feeling. What good is that? Don't you have a beeper?"

Martin shook his head.

"You should get one," Seymour said. "I don't know what I'd do without mine."

He pulled it out of its monogrammed leather case and handed it to Martin to admire.

"Tell you what," he continued. "After we eat, I'll take you over to Technilectrons and we'll pick out the best beeper on the market. What do you say to that?"

What could he say? Seymour was being so friendly and accommodating. Martin knew he'd have to overcome his agoraphobia (and quickly) if he wanted to make a good impression. He swallowed hard.

"How are the specials here?" he asked.

"Out of this world," Seymour replied. "Waiter, 2 cowpokes on the range. Medium." He winked at Martin. "I'm glad you found your appetite. Now you can be my prisoner. I want you to get acquainted with the complete Seymour Black." He laughed. "I love a captive audience."

Seymour started at the beginning and spoke with such panache that he held Martin spellbound for the duration of the meal. Martin didn't even notice that he was given a smaller steak. His usual (and often accurate) paranoid tendencies had been temporarily put on hold.

As Seymour recounted the entire gamut of his exploits, Martin felt, (if he had the right address) he could send away for a written transcript of Seymour's life. He didn't realize that address was printed right on Seymour's card.

"I don't care about accepted or acceptable behavior," Seymour said. "I'm on a mission. If I want something... If I need something, I have no barriers. I succeed. Period." He produced a copy of his obituary. "Here, read this."

Martin did so and was almost moved to tears. "I feel like I've lived your life."

"Then I guess we understand each other." Seymour grabbed the obituary from Martin and dramatically tore it up.

"What are you doing?" Martin said.

"An impulse. The way I feel about death, maybe. And anyway, it's just a copy. Remember this, Martin Mall," and he pointed to himself, "don't ever destroy the original."

17

After lunch the two men returned to Garden Park. Back in his element, Martin felt as if a tremendous pressure had been lifted from his shoulders. He was ready — almost excited — to resume his grind. But Seymour reminded him of the necessity to shop for a beeper.

"We'll take the top of the line," Seymour said to the sales clerk at Technilectrons. "Yes, this is it. I should know. I've got the exact same model." And to Martin, "I'll give you the name of a leather shop so you can get a nice carrying case, too. It's the little extras that make life worthwhile."

"I don't know what you told him," the sales clerk said, "but we've been trying to convince Mr. Mall here to buy one of our beepers for the last 6 months. He always put us off. Perhaps with your encouragement, he'll consent to appear in one of our testimonial flyers. With his beeper, of course."

"Not a bad idea," said Seymour...

"I don't do ads," Martin curtly replied. "It would compromise my position and the position of the mall. How much do I owe you?"

"Nada," Seymour answered. "It's on me."

"You really shouldn't," Martin said.

"Forget it. It's a gift."

Another gift? Martin couldn't believe it. First Sandy's lagniappe and now the Seymour beeper. He wasn't used to all the presents. Malls, he thought, are not a giving place.

"Thank you," he said. "I appreciate it. And thank you for lunch. If there's any way I can be of assistance, don't hesitate to..."

"How about a tour?" Seymour asked.

"Of course," Martin replied. "It's the least I can do."

Martin took Seymour all over the mall. The two of them had their pictures taken inside the photo booth, shaking hands with Chris. Martin apologized for the state of the center and explained the reason for the disarray: Garden Park was being completely revamped for the Grand Reopening and 25th Anniversary Celebrations. He spoke in intimate terms. He was undergoing the same kinds of changes as his mall.

Seymour barely heard him. He was having a self-actualization of his own. He remembered how many hours he had spent in Garden Park. Images from his past were bombarding his system. Everywhere he walked, he was reminded of himself. The young lawyer, defensive. The neophyte rabbi, trying to understand the humanity in a closed shopping bag. He'd been spending too much energy diversifying lately. He forgot what it felt like to be whole. And now here he was... is... will be... For the first time. Together under one roof.

"This mall is my conscience," he whispered. "This mall is my soul... I've got to reorient," Seymour continued. "Stop spreading myself so thin. The world is becoming a cancer. Malls are expanding disproportionately with the universe..."

"I beg your pardon."

"It's nothing," said Seymour. "I was just doing a bit of philosophizing."

"With your background, you probably do that a lot."

"Not like I used to," Seymour replied. "This mall seems to bring it out of me. But enough Seymour Black. Why don't you give me a glimpse into the inner workings of Martin Mall?"

Martin smiled shyly and started pointing — to the Garden, the shoppers, the stores...

"This is it," he said. "Everything you see right here."

"So you're a company man," Seymour said. "An admirable trait." He leaned toward him. "I was referring to your personal life."

Martin continued pointing...

"Uh-huh. You're holding back..."

Martin's pointing increased in intensity. Seymour was getting hot under the collar.

"You know Martin Mall," he said, "I expected more from you. I felt we were on the verge of a solid relationship. I spent the whole of our lunch exposing myself, treating you to a beeper..."

"I'm sorry," Martin said. "I didn't mean to offend you. It's just there isn't anything to my personal life that you can't see right here. Maybe there's something wrong with me. Maybe I'm one dimensional. But if that's the case, I'm very proud of my dimension."

"Certainly you must have a hidden dream," Seymour said. "Something in the back of your mind that doesn't relate directly to Garden Park."

"I suppose..."

"Now you're talking."

"It's ridiculous, really."

"No it's not. Go on," Seymour urged.

"I — I can't," Martin said. "As much as I'd like to, I just feel stupid saying it aloud."

"Martin Mall," said Seymour, "I've been to the edge. I've stood on so many precipices I no longer speculate on the length of the fall... Let it all hang out, dammit."

Martin wavered a moment, then made an effort.

"Ever since I was a little boy," he said, "I've been curious about my..." He stopped. "I know this sounds silly, but deep down I believed if I looked hard enough in the mall I'd be able to find..." He was choking back tears. "I'm sorry. It's too painful. I just can't talk about it."

"That's alright," said Seymour quietly. "At least you're trying."

I am, thought Martin. Seymour's so perceptive. And compassionate, too. And he did buy me this beeper. I wonder... Is it possible I'm standing face to face with... that this is the person I've been searching for... that Seymour Black is my long lost fath...

"How about we get back to me?" Seymour asked. "I have a fantastic project in the works."

Martin was jolted to reality. "Oh... yes. Let's save it for my office."

"Whatever you say," Seymour said. "You're the boss."

"In that case, maybe you wouldn't mind screening my pilot. I mean you are in show business."

"I didn't know you produced."

"I dabble," Martin said.

"Well, lead the way. For the rest of the afternoon I'm all yours, kid."

Kid, mused Martin. He called me his kid. He was almost tempted to say, OK, Dad. But he held himself back. Martin was letting the events of the day get too far out of hand.

18

Martin hesitated outside the door to his office. He wasn't in the mood for one of Peaches' scenes.

"Just give me a head start," he said to Seymour. "I promised my secretary I'd warn her before I brought anyone home."

He held his breath and tried to be casual. "Peaches, I'm back. Sorry I took so long at lunch. I completely lost track of time. I hope there were no emergencies. By the way, Seymour Black's going to stop by later this afternoon. Is that OK? Oh, and look what I got. A beeper. Now we'll always be able to keep in touch. Isn't that great, Peaches? Peaches..." Martin did a double take. It took him a moment to realize he was talking to an empty room. "You probably think I'm crazy," he said when Seymour came in, "but I expected to find my secretary here. She's usually very dependable."

"Don't worry," Seymour replied. "It's hard to find decent help nowadays. Besides, the way this office looks, you're better off without her."

Martin couldn't help but agree. File drawers were open, papers were everywhere. And Peaches' desk, which was always immaculate, was a certifiable disaster area. Martin didn't like it one bit. one bit.

"It's all wrong," he said. "Peaches never left an untidy room in her life. Maybe we've been vandalized by industrial spies. What if she's been kidnapped and held for ransom by a group of anti-mall terrorists?"

"Just relax," Seymour said. "You're letting your imagination get the best of you."

"No," said Martin. "You don't know Peaches. This isn't her style. Something terrible must have happened. I'd better call Mall Security."

"What's this?" Seymour asked, motioning to the machine on top of her desk.

"A dictaphone," Martin replied. "I bought it for her months ago. She never even tried it. She always put everything in writing."

"Why don't we turn it on?"

"There's no point. Peaches wouldn't dream of stooping to..."

But it was too late. Seymour had already switched it to play. The sound of a faint, distraught voice resonated through the speaker.

"Peaches..." Martin gasped.

"Testing. Testing," said Peaches on the tape. "I'm so embarrassed. I'm not even sure how this thing works. This is a memo to Martin Mall, from your secretary — correction, former secretary — Peaches del Muhne. 2 spaces. Hello. How are you? It's been brought to my attention... No. That's not right. I'm a complete loss without my white-out. Maybe I should improvise... Martin Mall, I hate you! You humiliated me. You ruined my reputation. You turned me into fourth class postage... There, I feel a little better..."

"Those are strong words," Seymour said. "Do you want me to shut it off?"

Martin let out a solitary sob. "No. Leave it on. I have to listen. I owe her that much."

"You're a brave man," Seymour replied.

"...Are you with me?"

Martin nodded and turned up the volume.

Peaches continued, "You made me lie, too. I didn't want to do it. I didn't want to do it. Oh my god. I'm sorry. I never burst into spontaneous song before, but then again, the past few weeks have been full of new experiences for me. I never felt incompetent, either. These days I seem to be an old hand at it. Thanks for the training, boss. A word of warning: The Merchants' Association is on the war path. They're too smart for your games. 4 missed meetings make a very strong statement and no one can tell me they're not being interpreted as such. Martin Mall, you don't seem to realize that running a mall is a collaborative art. That's all I have to say. And now, I bid you farewell. I'm going somewhere to put my files in order. Good-bye. End of memo. By the way, there was a call for you from the Lincoln Overview Head Office. They said it's urgent. The message is on your desk."

"Peaches," cried Martin, plaintively. "Where are you? I have to find her. I've got to lure her back. I'll beg her to return... Promise her anything. I'll change. I swear it."

"Get a hold of yourself," Seymour said. "You're falling apart. No employee is worth that much grief. One leaves, you find another. Simple as that."

"Peaches was more than an employee, she was like a mother to me."

"So maybe it's time you left home." Seymour reached inside a pocket and took out an address book. "I'll get you a Cheryl."

Cheryl was an agency's eponym for all their secretary/receptionists. It provided continuity. Painless replacement.

He picked up the receiver, made 2 quick calls and within half an hour a Cheryl arrived. Seymour put her to work, cleaning Peaches' mess, implementing her own filing system and answering Garden Park's phones.

"I don't know how to thank you," Martin said. "You've made the mall whole again."

"I take care of my own," said Seymour. "Think of me as your godfather."

God... Father... thought Martin, concretely. Was this additional evidence? Seymour triggered a fantasy that was beyond Martin's control.

"Do you have any family?" Martin blurted out.

"What do you mean?" Seymour was taken aback. "No, I don't have any to speak of. I was married once, but that's another story... I guess I'm just a solitary man, as Neil Diamond used to say. Or was it Neil Sedaka? I always get those two mixed up. I'm curious, though. Why do you ask?"

Martin blushed. Seymour was getting too close. Why is he baiting me, Martin wondered. He hated being vulnerable. That was one of the things he liked best about Garden Park. Only stores have to open up in a mall.

"I have a confession," said Seymour. "In the form of a parable."

Martin's heart skipped a beat. He was ready for an emotional catharsis.

"There once was a rabbi," Seymour began, "whose congregation was located across the street from a successful mall. And this rabbi used to visit the mall every Friday afternoon, trying to come up with ideas for his sermons. He felt there was something mystical there and if he could somehow harness that spirit it would guide him to the secrets of the universe. In fact, the mall never did fail to inspire the rabbi. Anyway, there was also a little boy who used to follow the rabbi around. The rabbi wasn't sure if this boy's mother shopped in the mall, or if his father owned one of the stores. For all he knew, the child was a permanent resident. In any event, the little boy fascinated the rabbi. He never walked with him, always 5 paces behind. And whenever the rabbi tried to make contact, the child disappeared..."

"I remember you," said Martin, "very clearly. You were such a mysterious figure. You never carried a shopping bag."

"Yes," Seymour replied. "That's because the stores didn't sell what I was buying. They still don't. So tell me, Martin, how did you interpret this mysterious figure? Did you ever imagine I might be someone special?"

Damn him, thought Martin. He must know. Surely, it's no coincidence that the only man to ask about my fantasy, is the same one who inspired it.

"Actually," he said, "I didn't imagine you to be anyone."

"Oh well, just curious. I guess I wanted to flatter myself. But that's irrelevant. It doesn't shed one iota of light on the reason I wanted to meet with you. Let me get to the point. Do you know what I always wanted more than anything else?"

Martin tried to hide his excitement. "No, who... uh... what?"

"Immortality," Seymour replied. "The only thing my life is missing. Not for long, though. I think I may have found it."

"Where?"

"Look around you."

"You mean Garden Park?"

"Precisely," Seymour said. "Martin Mall, I'd like to tell you a parable."

"Another one?" asked Martin.

"I'm on a roll," Seymour said. "I told you this place inspires me. Do you want to hear it, or not?"

"Of course I do."

"Fine." He took a moment to pause for effect. "Many years ago, after the destruction of the Temple in Jerusalem, a number of scholars and religious leaders wanted to spruce up the Wailing Wall, make it fancy, give it a little class. So they got together... formed committees... talked... argued... wrote reports... But it wasn't happening. They couldn't reach a consensus. Until finally an innocent young girl visits the Wall and leaves behind a gift, a tiny potted plant. And it looked terrific next to all that exposed brick. The elders called it a miracle. Their prayers had been answered. They consulted a decorator, placed an order and 40 years later... the Wandering Jews arrived. Do you see what I'm getting at?"

Martin shook his head. He was thinking about how well Seymour would relate to the Wandering Customer.

"Open your eyes, man," Seymour bellowed. "I am that plant. I am the quintessential Wandering Jew!"

"So why don't you settle in Israel?"

"That's not the point. Nowadays everyone's a Wandering Jew. People are always moving — from place to place, job to job..."

"Mall to mall," Martin interjected.

"Mall to mall," Seymour replied. "But the buck stops here. It's been 15 years since I've been back to Garden Park. And even though everything's different, everything's ultimately the same. Malls are survivors. What mall has gone bankrupt? What mall has closed down? Malls are forever. If that's not immortality, I don't know what is."

"I couldn't have put it better myself," Martin said.

"Before I came here," said Seymour, "I was going to develop my own mall. I've already picked out the property. I wanted you to join me as my right hand man. The road to immortality always needs a right hand man. Then you showed me around and what you suggested earlier, about buying Garden Park hit me where it counts. It's so simple. I have no other choice. I'm bound to this place in a way I can't quite explain. This mall knows me, better than I know myself."

"This mall knows everything," Martin said.

"Amen," Seymour replied. "Well Martin, the offer still stands. I have complete faith in you... in us... as a team. Are you with me?"

Martin stood there beaming.

"Welcome aboard," Seymour continued. "So, who owns this mall?"

"The Lincoln Overview Development Corporation. Lincoln O.D. Are you familiar with them?" Martin asked.

"Not personally," Seymour answered. "But I suppose I will be soon enough. Now when do we see that pilot of yours? And what kind of program is it?"

"A talk show," said Martin.

"All talk, no action," Seymour mumbled.

"I'm sorry?"

"An industry joke... What's it called?"

"Garden Party."

"Good. It's a 2 word title with a strong sense of space. Those are key elements. That adds up to success in my books." Seymour noticed Martin fidgeting. "Is something wrong?"

"It's just that you're a professional and I'm so new at this. I'm a little embarrassed about my work."

"There's no need for that," Seymour said. "You may be a beginner to the world of showbiz, but I'm a beginner to the world of malls. Together we have experience to share."

How could Martin refute logic like that? He pulled out the tape, turned on the cassette and started the show on the road.

Seymour concentrated on the screen. "Good beginning," he said. "That's very important."

Yes, thought Martin, imagining father and son at the helm of a mall. It is a good beginning.

19

At 9:28 p.m. the emergency lines started ringing all over Garden Park. An urgent Merchants' Association meeting had been called. Unfortunately, hardly anyone was around the answer their phones because so few of the stores were open.

This didn't bother Calvin Dighby and Susan Carlyle, the perpetrators of the action. They were prepared for a shoddy turnout. It was part of their plan. They were dealing with a delicate matter and the fewer people involved the better.

Several hours earlier, Calvin declared the mall to be in a state of emergency. He used his presidential powers to invoke martial law. As a show of strength he subcontracted a security force (in the name of the Association), while he and Susan drafted resolutions dispensing (temporarily) with their democratic regime. They instituted an oligarchy (for the good of the mall, of course) and suspended the constitution. Every merchant in attendance would automatically be made an ad hoc member of a special regulatory committee. It would be their duty to supervise the reinstatement of free elections when the time was right.

These measures were typed, xeroxed and handed out to the dozen or so retailers who managed to attend. Chris was there, too. As an observer. He was carrying a loaded instamatic camera. Calvin asked him to be the documentarian.

"I tried to get video," Chris said. "But I don't have a credit card and couldn't make the cash deposit."

The meeting took place in a store called the Hot Tub, a trendy upscale Turkish steambath. According to its owners, Enzo and Tullio Smyth-Jones, it was a prototype for more to come. Enzo and Tullio were a pair of fussy fraternal twins whose work garb consisted of pastel colored togas. Actually, the brothers weren't always called Enzo and Tullio. Their names used to be Eric and Todd, but they felt the Italian gave their establishment a certain je ne sais quoi.

The merchants were clad in Hot Tub trunks and tops and were lounging in their choice of unscented or strawberry-banana whirlpools. (Strawberry-banana was the scent of the week.) They were trying to read the Calvin Manifesto without getting it too wet. Only Calvin and Susan wouldn't participate. They were still wearing their street clothes. They felt the water took away from the dignity of the proceedings.

Here is a list of the members in attendance who formed the ad hoc regulatory committee:
Calvin Dighby, President
Susan Carlyle, Vice-President
Enzo and Tullio Smyth-Jones, Secretary and Treasurer, respectively
Edgar Portlee, Portlee Designatore Inc.
Harry Rodd, Sheer Curtains
Fair Deal Jake Savitt, from the car dealership of the same name
Becky Melloh, Manager of Wright-Ellis, "fine clothes for fine people"
Mike Serfino, Manager of the Record Rack
Irving Oscar Jr., owner of Creative Juices, a health beverage kiosk that also sells food processors
Chris, Ex-officio

Enzo and Tullio were running around, passing out the snacks they had graciously prepared.
"Would anyone like another danish?" Enzo said. "Or perhaps an avocado brioche?"
"Don't be shy," said Tullio. "We have plenty more in the back."
"You boys custom cater now, don't you?" Susan Carlyle asked.
"We sure do," Tullio replied.
"We'll come out to your home and fill your tubs with all sorts of goodies," Enzo continued. "You just have to book us 6 weeks in advance."
"And after the meeting," Tullio said, "you're invited to peruse our catalogue of aquatic delights."
"Our wet dream," Enzo added.
The two of them giggled in a chorus.
"Can I have your attention?" Calvin shouted impatiently. "We have a lot of important business to discuss. You can indulge in all the shop-talk you want when we finish." He cleared his throat 3 times. He didn't have a gavel and thought the act of clearing was the next best thing. "I call this meeting to order. Welcome. In a time of crisis it's a very reassuring sight to see familiar faces. It reaffirms my faith in retail. Even 1 kiosk showed up and that makes me doubly happy, considering he only gets half a vote. But tonight is a night where every half vote counts. Like our motto says, 'We are links in a retail chain'."
Calvin proudly pointed to the Merchants' Association banner,

which had been hung on the wall behind the president's chair. "I think we can dispense with the formalities," Calvin said, "and get down to brass tacks. Could I please have a motion to that effect."

"I move we ignore Robert's Rules of Order," said Fair Deal Jake Savitt.

"I second the motion," Enzo replied.

"You can't second a motion in your own establishment," Tullio said. "It's not polite."

"You're out of order, Tullio," Calvin said.

"Don't call my brother out of order," Enzo snapped. "Or I'll take back my second."

"I'm sorry," Calvin answered. "Can we go on?"

"Just because I stuck up for you," Enzo said to his brother, "doesn't mean I think you're in the right."

"Why don't we consult Robert's Rules of Order," Tullio suggested.

"We've thrown them out," grumbled Fair Deal Jake.

"Not yet," Susan replied. "It hasn't gone to vote. So if anyone wants to make another motion..."

"Order," Calvin said. "Can I please have some order." With the merchants talking and the whirlpools going full blast, he could barely be heard above the din.

When Sandy arrived there was such a commotion that she was able to slip in unnoticed and take her rightful place next to her father.

"Sorry I'm late," she said. "I was with a customer."

"What did I tell you?" Harry whispered to Edgar.

"Did I miss anything?" Sandy asked.

"Nothing important," Harry answered.

"You'll like this Merchants' Association," Edgar said. "They're a lively bunch."

"Want a danish?" Enzo asked Sandy.

"No thanks," she replied.

Calvin was desperate. "People. Hello? Don't you have any respect for our motto? Or maybe it's me. Maybe you don't think I'm a capable leader. Which is it? If you want me to resign, just say the word. We'll have a vote of confidence. I'm ready to step down. I ask not what my mall can do for me..."

"Alright Calvin, there's no need for hysterics," Edgar said. Edgar was past-president of the Merchants' Association. "Would everyone pipe down and let Calvin run this meeting. I, for one, have a lot to do in the morning and I don't want this thing running all night."

Murmurs of "So do I"; "You're right"; "Me too"; echoed through the group. In a moment, they were quiet.

"There Calvin," Edgar continued, "is that better?"

Calvin shrugged and made a face.

For the next few minutes everyone tried to pay attention to the proceedings. They had to listen very carefully. Calvin had worn his throat raw from shouting and was having problems getting the words out. If it weren't for the Mr. Microphone Enzo produced, he wouldn't have been heard at all.

"Until now," Calvin said, "we were dreamers. We were laughed at and discouraged. People accused us of paranoia and told us to get our heads out of the clouds and back to our markups. But did we listen? Do paranoids ever listen? No, my friends, we did not! And while we may have acted foolishly — turned our backs on reason — it was our very foolishness that is saving us from the horrors of a totalitarian mall. My friends, or should I call you my partners? For that is what we are. We are about to embark on a magnificent journey, from slavery unto freedom. Let me quote from the Jewish Passover service: 'Why is this night different from all other nights?' On all other nights, the Merchants' Association is responsible to mall management. Tonight, we are the management. Down with the Martin Mall's of the world, who seek to dominate and control us. Up with the world's first condominium mall development!"

Calvin began chanting, "Go condo, go condo, go condo," expecting everyone to join in.

They didn't.

"Calvin, is all this... separation talk really necessary?" asked Edgar.

"Yes," said Becky Melloh of the Wright-Ellis outlet. "Now that we've shown Martin Mall we mean business, can't we back off?"

"This is where negotiations come in," said Fair Deal Jake. "They make an offer. We counter with another one..."

"Don't be such a car dealer," Tullio said.

"Man, I'm with Jake," said Mike Serfino of the Record Rack. "I'm not sure my head office is willing to go all the way. Self-government is a heavy scene."

"This is crazy," said Creative Juices' Irving Oscar Jr. "Where's our pioneer spirit? Who are we? Merchants or mice?"

"Please calm down," said Enzo. "What will the neighbors think?"

"Don't be ignorant," Susan replied. "We are the neighbors."

Pretty soon everyone was talking. Opinions were challenged. Factions formed. Anarchy was setting in. Calvin had lost control and there was nothing he could do to regain it. His voice was gone. He just sat there making be quiet charades. But no one paid any attention. They simply thought he'd developed another nervous twitch.

All of a sudden, the chaos was silenced by a scream. A woman, resembling a bag lady, stepped up to the podium and started to speak. "I bet you're surprised to see me."

It was Peaches del Muhne and she was obviously in a state. Her hair-do was dishevelled, her outfit, lopsided. Her makeup was running down the sides of her face and dripping on her collar.

Calvin cringed. Peaches' appearance was certainly no testimony to the durability of his designs.

"First of all," she said. "I must apologize to Calvin Dighby, who spent at least 45 minutes yesterday fixing my hair. This isn't your fault, Calvin. I did this to myself. It's my penance. Today I committed the most heinous sin a secretary is capable of. I turned my back on a mess. Most of you who know me, realize I spent my entire life in the pursuit of organization. So you'll all agree that only the most dire circumstances would provoke me to such extremes. I blame Martin Mall. He destroyed me and he's in the process of destroying you. I hate to tell you this, because Martin's been like a son to me. But this shopping center has been my family. And the way I see it, how can I sacrifice my whole family for one sick member? The only chance you have of saving yourselves from this cancer, is to rally around Calvin and buy out Garden Park. You have no time to lose. Go condo, go condo, go..." She left the podium in tears.

"Go condo, go condo, go condo." The merchants picked up the chant. They rose to their feet, climbed out of their whirlpools and dried themselves off. Then they linked arms and began swaying to the rhythm. The Hot Tub was really cooking.

Calvin, mustering all the saliva he had, moistened his tonsils and said, "I think we owe a debt of gratitude to this wonderful lady." He pointed to Peaches. "I move we make her an honorary merchant of Garden Park."

A half dozen seconds were shouted from the group. Peaches was hoisted from where she stood and paraded like a monarch around the room. Someone found a sale banner and pinned it to her arm. The mood was jubilant, but intense. The ad hoc regulatory committee had transformed itself into a cult.

"Let me have your attention." Calvin's voice was back. "We still have plenty of details to iron out before we announce our formal bid tomorrow morning. I can't wait to see Martin Mall's face when he hears he's been dismissed by our new cooperative. That'll teach him he can't mess with retail and get..."

"Excuse me," Sandy interrupted. "Can I say something?"

"By all means," Calvin replied. "This is your mall, too. Ladies and gentlemen, I give the floor to Sandy Rodd from the new Sheer Curtains outlet. We're proud to have her as part of our team. Although I will admit, I had a few reservations about whose side she would actually be on. Nevertheless, her presence here this evening, despite her obvious lateness, shows us where her heart is. Sandy, would you prefer to speak from your tub, or ascend to the podium?" Calvin asked.

"Right here will be fine." She fidgeted. "You know, it's a funny thing. When it comes to customers I'm never at a loss for words. But tonight, I feel a little nervous. Maybe if I pass out a few cards..."

She found her purse, produced a stack of business cards and circulated them around the room.

"There," said Sandy. "That's better. And in case you're interested, these cards are worth an extra 15% discount at any Sheer Curtains location. Anyway, I wanted to tell you that this condo thing is a great idea. And I'm all for it. I just don't like... I mean, won't you give Martin a chance to explain himself in person?"

"Sandy's got a point," Edgar interjected.

"We gave him more chances than he's worth," said Susan Carlyle. "And the son-of-a-gun never even had the courtesy to show up."

"I'm going to terminate this discussion," Calvin said. "There's too much on the agenda. All those in favor of removing Martin Mall from the new Garden Park, say aye..."

"I can't believe my ears," said Sandy.

"Well, well," Susan replied, "your true colors are showing. Exactly how many lunches did you and Martin have? And of course, we can't forget those midnight trysts. Shall we let everyone in on the details?"

"That's absurd," Sandy said. "I'm a professional."

"We never doubted that," Susan shot back.

"I refuse to submit to this kind of slander. And if you must know, I met with Martin to sell him drapes for his office and that was all!" Sandy grabbed her belongings and stormed out of the meeting.

"If you've got nothing to hide," Susan called, "why are you running away... And don't think the entire business community isn't going to hear about your actions... you traitor... you wholesaler in retailer's clothing..."

"Stop! I beg you, please stop!" It was Harry Rodd. "I don't know what's come over Sandy. She was never like this growing up. But I want to assure you the Rodds are retail stock, through and through. We have 85 stores and 22 in development and this is the first time a Sheer Curtains' Rodd ever walked out on a Merchants' Association. I'm so ashamed. Please forgive her actions. She will be dealt with later. I am still the president of Sheer Curtains. What I say goes. I want it on record that my company supports the actions of the Garden Park Merchants' Association — 100%."

20

After her exchange with the Merchants' Association, Sandy retreated to the safety of her store.

"I was wrong about this mall," she explained to the samples. "Selling means nothing to them. They're into power."

She abhorred that mentality. Sandy wished she had never heard of Garden Park, never set foot in its warped establishment. Her only solace was the fact that there would be other outlets to breathe into life. Sandy wouldn't let one rotten apple spoil her whole retail bunch.

She took a good hard look around her. Everything was perfect, not a unit out of place. From chaos came forth order. From darkness came forth light. From samples came forth sales.

At least that was how it was supposed to happen...

She tried improvising orders, but she couldn't keep her mind on it. She was restless. She wanted to get back at the Merchants' Association. She didn't care about the risk, she had a personal vendetta to settle.

Sandy decided to warn Martin. It was the least she could do. Once a deposit had been secured, she always protected her customers. She called Martin at his office and let the phone ring 10 or 11 times. That's strange, she thought, he doesn't usually leave the mall.

She scanned the phonebook for his home number. Her effort proved in vain. The directory listed many malls, but none that began with the given name Martin.

"I should've expected it," Sandy said. "Why would anyone as close to celebrity status as Martin take the chance of listing himself in so public a medium? You never know how many nuts are dying to get hold of him."

She made a mental note to have her name stricken from the phonebooks of the 14 Sheer Curtains cities.

Sandy replayed the events of the evening. She was starting to doubt her actions. Why did she speak out? Was she in the wrong? Did she betray her tribe? She wasn't sure any more. She felt guilty and alone. She stiffened. A case of depression had just been delivered. It was unloaded in the middle of her back. It caused a sharp pain which made her wince. She sat down and attempted to regain control of her situation.

What am I going to do? she wondered. I suppose I could

apologize to the Merchants' Association. But I do have my pride. I could search for Martin, except I haven't a clue where to begin. I hate this store. I need out. Maybe it's a sign — to give up retail. It's such a dirty game... I could go back to school... become a civil servant... get a job in the media. I have a few contacts. That could lead somewhere... Which way am I going, Willy?

Sandy went on like this for over 2 hours, until a noise outside the store broke her concentration. She peered through the window and saw Martin Mall.

He seemed preoccupied. Every so often he dialed a number on one of the pay phones. He'd wait a moment, smile with glee and then jump happily up and down.

His behavior surprised Sandy. She couldn't understand the point of wasting so much money on the calls, when his office was just upstairs.

"Martin," she said.

He didn't hear her. Sandy left the store. She followed him to every pay phone in the mall. She tried to make contact, but he wouldn't respond. He was in another world.

Not knowing what to do, Sandy headed for the garden and flopped down on Martin's favorite bench.

It was almost 5:00 a.m. and the mall was an eerie place. Even though it was completely enclosed, a damp mist pervaded the area and the synthetic leaves were wet with plastic dew.

"Nice effect, isn't it?"

Sandy jumped. It was Martin Mall. She hadn't noticed him sneaking up on her.

"Haven't we met?" he asked.

"Martin," she said, "I've been watching your telephone routine. What on earth has got into you?"

Martin was oblivious to Sandy's remarks. "The reason for the mist," he said, "is that it gives the mall reality. Why else would these plants seem so alive? Do you think people would come here on days when they had no intention of shopping, just to bask in a garden surrounded by phonies? Not a chance. That's why we had to do something special. So we have atmospheric conditions piped in, 24 hours a day. Like muzak, only much more subtle."

"Martin, I'm trying to help you."

He ignored her. He pulled a little black box from his pocket and displayed it for Sandy with the enthusiasm of a child.

"Do you know what this is?" he asked.

"Of course," she said a little annoyed. "It's a beeper."

"Do you have one?"

"No... Yes. It's being repaired. What does that have to do with..."

"Come with me," he said and he darted into the mall.

Sandy was close behind. She was becoming increasingly concerned about Martin. She knew how obsessed he'd been with the anniversary celebrations and his TV show, so she decided to humor him.

They stopped at a pay phone.

"Watch," he said. He was trembling uncontrollably.

He deposited a coin, dialed a number and then waited for the connection to be made. All of a sudden, his black box was beeping and beeping and beeping. The noise stopped abruptly when Martin hung up.

"What do you make of it?" he asked.

"Your machine has a short circuit," she replied. "It shouldn't be doing what it's doing. And for that matter neither should you. I think you both need an overhaul."

"You don't understand," said Martin. And he began to sing, "You don't understand... you don't understand..."

He ran off to another phone and repeated his routine. Sandy was right on his tail.

"Martin, I..."

"Can't you see," he said. "I'm being called."

"It's just a mistake."

"Do you have any idea who gave me this beeper?"

"I'm afraid I don't."

"Seymour gave it to me," Martin replied. "Seymour Black. He's a holy man. Not only that, he's my father. My long, lost father."

"Your what? Who told you this?"

"No one had to tell me," Martin said. "I figured it out myself... in one of my visions."

"Martin, we all fantasize. That doesn't mean..." She held herself back. She remembered Willy and the joy of being born again. How many people would have called that idle daydreaming? She began to see Martin in a new light. There was another reason for this. A reddish-yellow glow was enveloping the mall.

"C'mon," said Martin. "I want to catch the sunrise."

Sunrise? Sandy wondered where the skylight was.

"There is no skylight," he said, reading her thought. "Let's go, or we'll miss the best part. I'll fill you in on my vision when we get there... Hurry."

"I'm hurrying," she said, "I'm hurrying."

Sunrise in Garden Park was a magnificent sight. A computerized dimmer system controlled the illumination. Orange gels enhanced the effect. And the faint sounds of chirping birds had been added to the muzak. The air was electric with anticipation. Sandy had never seen anything so breathtaking in her life.

"You've been out in the world. You've seen other malls," Martin said, out of the blue. "Tell me, what are they like?"

"Most malls are pretty much the same," she replied.

"But not this one. Garden Park's special, isn't it?"

The question caught Sandy off guard. She hesitated. Martin answered for her. "Of course it is," he said. "Garden Park's going to be famous... Did anyone ever tell you how the garden got its smell?"

"You did," she said.

"Oh. Then you already know. I wanted to explain it to you. It's a wonderful story."

"Well," said Sandy, "I wouldn't mind if you told me the story again. But I'd prefer to hear about your vision."

"My vision," said Martin. "Oh, yes. My vision. Alright. Are you a creative person?"

"My card says I am and I sold you some drapes."

"I guess that qualifies," he replied. "I'm only allowed to share my visions with the truly creative. No one else is able to understand... I think my brain has taken a vacation. Do you ever feel that?"

Sandy didn't know what to say. She was genuinely worried about Martin's state of mind.

"Earlier this evening," he continued, "I was alone in my office... meditating... tossing a few ideas around. I do that a lot because of the anniversary, the Grand Reopening, my show and everything. I decided I wouldn't let myself be distrubed for any reason short of catastrophe. After a while, I felt myself dozing. I never fell asleep, though. Not really. I always knew I could wake up at any instant. If I wanted to. But I didn't. I encouraged myself to drift... past everything that's happened in the last few weeks. And no matter how hard I tried, each thought led me back to my glorious day with Seymour. That's not strange, is it? After all, we are old friends. He used to be a rabbi who came here for inspiration. I suspect it was me who inspired him. Anyway, I was floating. And I remembered my past. I think I mentioned this when we first met, that when I heard you worked with your father, I was so envious. I never knew my father. I used to imagine that any man I passed was my dad. Dad. It's such a funny sounding word. Dadadadada... I always prayed for the day that fate would thrust my father back into my life. And now it's happening, exactly the way I planned. I'm on the verge of a turning point. I can feel it. I have visions, you know."

"I know," she replied, "I know. I know."

"And tonight's..." he said. "Seymour was everywhere. And I was inside him. Inside and out at the very same time. I heard the voices in his head. He was a troubled man. I heard the voices tell him what to do. And I saw a tear in his eye the day he opened the door to his sleeping son's bedroom and watched him lying there, so peaceful and calm. And Seymour said, 'No... I can't... Never. Never. Never!' But the voices in his head persisted and he couldn't refuse any longer. He picked up his child, being ever so careful not to disturb him and carried him across the street to the center of a deserted mall. I don't blame Seymour. He didn't enjoy it. He was being tested. He placed his little boy on a mound of astroturf. Seymour was crying quite openly. He kissed his baby and left. But he didn't forget him. He dropped by every week. As the little boy grew, Seymour spoke to him less and less, until finally the pain became too much to bear. And he was forced to leave his house, his congregation and his son. Sandy do you have any idea who that little boy was? That little boy was me!"

Sandy was shivering. All the color had disappeared from her cheeks.

"Martin," she said, "that was a vivid... dream and I don't want to put a damper on it... What I mean is, Seymour may be a lot of things. I'd be the first to admit that. But he wouldn't abandon his only child."

"He didn't abandon me," Martin corrected. "He sacrificed me to the mall. He had no choice. He had to sacrifice me in order to be redeemed. And I did redeem him. It was me who brought him back to his Promised Land. This afternoon, Seymour gave me a present. A beeper. That was the straw that broke the camel's back. This tiny machine convinced me that Seymour was my father. A few hours ago, I was frightened by my telephone. It awakened me. It rang and rang and rang. And while it was ringing a miracle occurred. My beeper started beeping and wouldn't stop. It took me a few minutes to realize that this was the link between Seymour and me; the link between father and son. I was so thrilled, I let my beeper beep for almost half an hour. Then I ran into the mall, to make absolutely sure I wasn't deluding myself. I kept experimenting with different pay phones. And the machine didn't disappoint me once."

Sandy was speechless. She just sat on the bench and stared at Martin's beeper. As hard as she tried, she couldn't resist wanting to believe his story. Only the recollection of the Merchants' Association brought her back to her senses.

"Martin," she said, "you've got to do something. They're plotting against you."

"Who is?" he asked.

"The Merchants' Association. They're taking over Garden Park."

"Sandy," Martin said, "after everything I told you... They're a little ticked off because I broke a few appointments, that's all. I couldn't help it. I had more important things on my agenda."

"But Peaches said..."

Martin was stunned. "Peaches? You saw Peaches? How is she? Did she ask about me? Is she alright? I knew Peaches wouldn't let me down. Even after she left today. I knew I could count on her to defend me."

Sandy wasn't about to tell him the news.

"You've got to protect yourself," she said. "It may already be too late."

"Sandy, Sandy, Sandy. The Merchants' Association cannot evict me from my own home. And Garden Park is my home. Besides, Seymour, I mean, Dad, is buying me the mall. He gave me his word."

Oh my god, she thought. What is Seymour up to? And how does Sheer Curtains fit into all of this?

"Are you positive?" she asked.

Martin nodded.

"You know," she said, "the Merchants' Association is meeting at 8:00 a.m. to finalize the takeover arrangements." She bit her lip. "If Seymour's going to make his move, that will have to be the time."

"You're right," he said. "Maybe you'll accompany me to the festivities."

Sandy didn't answer. She closed her eyes and tried to think. Seymour buying the mall? Impossible. It was too ridiculous to be true. This was simply Martin's fantasy, his last ditch effort to save his position. She felt a pang of sorrow. But her sorrow quickly changed to anxiety. And Sandy wondered whether insanity was sufficient grounds for cancelling an order of drapes.

21

The members of Garden Park's ad hoc regulatory committee were motionless. They seemed frozen. They gathered that morning in Calvin's Penny Lane. Each retailer was wearing a specially designed Merchants' Association cape (a modified hairdressing smock). They had serious looks on their faces, pens in their hands and were huddled in a semi-circle around Calvin and Susan.

They were posing for the official signing the declaration photograph. It was Calvin's intention to commission an artist to turn the snapshot into a portrait. Then he'd have it made into numbered prints and present one to every store in the self-governing mall. The original would be placed on permanent display in the center of the garden (soon to be renamed "Retail Square").

"Just hold still for another minute," Chris said. "I know the flash will go off this time."

Chris was having technical difficulties. And people were losing their patience. He suggested squeezing everyone into the photo booth.

"I'm just not used to portable equipment," he said.

But it wasn't a viable alternative.

When Sandy and Martin arrived at Penny Lane, Martin barged right up to Calvin and spoiled the last shot on Chris' film.

"You've done it again Martin Mall," said Calvin. "Your timing's impeccable."

Martin mistook his cynicism for sincerity, glanced over at Sandy and winked. Sandy cringed. Martin looked around the salon and caught a glimpse of Peaches sitting alone in a corner. He waved his beeper at her, but Peaches pretended she didn't see him.

"If you don't mind," Martin said, "I'd like to address the meeting. Merchants, I want you to know I wasn't avoiding you on purpose. It's just that I've been very busy lately planning the Grand Reopening and 25th Anniversary Celebrations. *Our* celebrations, I might add. And I guess I got carried away. So no hard feelings. OK?"

The merchants shuffled uncomfortably. Calvin sensed a mood of conciliation. He realized he was in danger of losing everything.

"That's a lovely sentiment," he said to Martin. "But the damage has been done and it's a little late to repent. So if *you* don't mind, we have a lot of business to attend to before we open this mall. Would someone please run out and buy some film?" he asked.

Enzo and Tullio eagerly volunteered.

"Excuse me," Martin said. "I haven't finished."

"I'm afraid you have," Calvin replied. "You are no longer Martin Mall. We've stripped you of your title. We're grooming Chris to take over your position. You have no rights any more. You are an official nothing."

"That's a low blow," Martin said.

"Just a second," said Irving Oscar Jr. "This is a democratic regime. Martin should be granted his final request."

"Maybe we could have a motion to that effect," Fair Deal Jake suggested. He immediately proposed one.

After a brief discussion and a quick vote, Martin won the right to air his views by a small, but respectable majority.

"Fine," said Calvin, "you win. The merchants want you to have your say. And I must step aside and accept their decision."

"Thank you Calvin," Martin said. "And merchants, thank you for your undying support. It won't go unnoticed. I want to publicly declare that I forgive each and every one of you. I heard about my impending fate and the attempted take over of the mall..."

All eyes turned to Sandy and glared.

"I hate to be a stick in the mud," Martin continued, "but your revolution's not going to happen. I know retail inside and out. That's why you failed. I had a counter plan before you even started. And I'll let you in on a little secret, I have it on good authority that I'm going to be around for a long, long time. Now I have a surprise for you... Probably the biggest surprise of your lives..."

Martin paused to take a breath. He was shaking and sweating all over. Still, he couldn't stop for more than an instant. He'd gathered too much momentum. He had to keep going.

"Seymour Black is my father!" he bellowed.

Who? they wondered. Not one merchant dared say a word.

"Did you hear me?" he asked. "I said Seymour Black is my father. Do any of you have the slightest notion where my daddy is right now?"

The collective sadly shook their heads. They didn't know what to do. Sandy and Peaches were crying.

"I'll tell you where he is," Martin shouted. "He's buying me a present. He always buys me presents. See the beeper?" He held it up. "This is what he bought me yesterday. Know what he's getting me today?" Martin pointed to the floor. "Garden Park... Very shortly," he said, "it will all be mine. Well... mine and dad's. I'm not greedy. So where is he? He should be here soon. I'm such a lucky son. I can't wait to introduce him to you. My father... Seymour Black..."

"Did someone mention my name?"

"Hi dad," Martin said.

Seymour was so busy pushing through the crowd that he didn't notice Martin's greeting. He edged his way to the front of the room and motioned for silence.

"Ladies and gentlemen," said Seymour, "your attention please. I have an announcement."

He smiled. It felt good to be in front of a congregation again. Seymour hadn't realized how much he missed it.

"Ladies and gentlemen," Martin broke in, "I'd like to present a unique individual and a terrific guy... My father... Seymour Black." Martin was the only one who applauded.

"Your what?"

"You heard me."

"I'm not your... Where did you get such a preposterous idea?" Seymour asked. "Or is this some type of joke?" Seymour chuckled. "I have no children," he said. "The buck stopped here."

"But yesterday when we were together," said Martin, "I never felt closer to anyone in my life."

Seymour shrugged. "I had a nice time, too. You're a good kid."

"See," said Martin, "I told you..."

"Hold on," said Seymour, "you're being too interpretive."

"What's wrong? Are you ashamed to admit I'm your son?"

Martin hit a nerve.

"I'm not ashamed of anything," Seymour replied. "Not a single decision in my life. I have nothing to hide. You're not my child and that is that. Sorry to be so dogmatic. We can still be friends."

Martin's face was burning. A wave of nausea undulated through his body.

"You don't look so well," Seymour said. "Maybe you'd better lie down."

"I don't understand," Martin mumbled. "My vision... the miracle... it all made sense... I don't understand..."

Martin's temples were throbbing. He was conscious of only one thing. He had to escape from the Hot Tub. Now.

22

Seymour organized a group of volunteers, including Sandy Rodd and Fair Deal Jake, to search for Martin Mall.

"I'll join you as soon as I can," he said. "I still have some business to attend to." He paused. His eyes were watering. "We've just witnessed a very sad moment in a human being's life. And one for which we're all partly to blame..."

"Blame nothing," Calvin interrupted. "I knew he wasn't fit to be running this mall. Well, what are you waiting for — Enzo, Tullio, get the film." He addressed the merchants. "While they're gone there are 1 or 2 things we should iron out." He began reading the condominium proposal. "If there are any changes speak now," he said, "or forever hold your lease."

"I don't know who you are," said Seymour, "but please... shut up! I have something important to say."

"I happen to be Calvin Dighby, President of the Merchants' Association. And this is my store."

"Big deal," Seymour replied.

"Well I never..." Calvin said. "Mr. Black, I don't know where you got your credentials, but we're not used to this kind of insubordination in Garden Park."

"Here, here..." Susan added.

"Harry, do you want to identify me?" Seymour asked. "Or shall I flash a card."

"He's Chairman of my Board," Harry answered, "among other things."

"So you're part of the Sheer Curtains conspiracy," Calvin said.

"In a manner of speaking."

"It figures. You're a troublemaker — like your underling, Sandy Rodd. You should both be ashamed of yourselves, conniving with a lowlife like Martin Mall. You're a disgrace to retail, Mr. Black. I'm afraid that a model shopping center like ours has no room for one of your outlets. I'd like someone to entertain a motion that will have Sheer Curtains packing by closing time today."

"I entertain such a motion," said Susan Carlyle.

Seymour was losing his patience. "If you two would stop entertaining, maybe you'd see that your act is over and the curtain is already down. I'm not going to beat around the bush. Ladies and gentlemen, I just finished negotiating the deal. I own Garden Park." He pulled out an envelope. "Here..."

Seymour passed around his bill of sale to the remnants of the ad hoc regulatory committee. The merchants read it. They didn't hide their hurt. By the time it reached Calvin, he was so upset he tried to tear it up.

"Won't do you any good," Seymour said. "It's a copy."

Enzo and Tullio burst in. "We got the film," Enzo said.

"We found a convenience store that was having a sale," Tullio continued. "We bought 2 rolls."

Their enthusiasm was abruptly doused.

"Pipe down," Calvin snapped.

Seymour attempted to lighten the situation. "Hey," he said, "it's not the end of the world. I wasn't planning to raise your rents."

"Less than 24 hours ago," Calvin's voice was mournful, almost a chant, "I was speaking to our contact... at Lincoln Overview... and they assured me all systems were go... there were no other offers... I was Christopher Columbus... this mall was the Nina... the Pinta... the Santa Maria... under one roof..."

"Mr. Dighby," Seymour said, "you fail to grasp the fact that my offer didn't come in until late yesterday afternoon."

"But how..."

"Very simple," Seymour replied. "I told Lincoln Overview I would exceed your final bid by 15%."

"That's cheating," Calvin squeaked. "We spent a month working out this plan and you come along and spoil everything in 1 day."

"If the whole world was created in a week," Seymour said, "for a little thing like buying a mall, you've got to be impulsive."

"Isn't it against the International Shopping Center code for a retailer to own more than double their square footage in any given mall?" asked Susan Carlyle.

"You never give up," said Seymour. "But neither do I, Ms. Carlyle. Now if I'm not mistaken, the answer is yes. The thing is I'm no longer a retailer. At least I won't be very soon. This morning I had my lawyer draw up a contract selling Sheer Curtains back to Harry Rodd. I have the terms for you to look over, Harry. I'm sure you'll find them most agreeable."

"Seymour," said Harry. "I'm touched."

"Well," Seymour said, "I've taken more time than I hoped. It's after 10:00 and we're a half hour late opening my mall. Better get to your stores. I'm going to see if Martin's alright."

Seymour headed for the door.

"Mr. Black, please wait. I'd like to talk to you."

"Not now," said Seymour.

"I'm Peaches," said the woman.

"Martin's ex-secretary," he replied. "If it's about your old job, I'm sorry I can't help you. Running the place is still Martin's domain..."

"It's not that," she said. "I'm leaving Garden Park for good. But before I do, I want to give you something." She handed him a large leather bound black book. "It's the mall's 5-year plan. This is the future, Mr. Black. Yours and Martin's. Don't destroy it."

With that, she was gone.

Seymour noticed a flurry of activity and pointed himself in the direction of the garden. They must have found Martin, he thought. They must have found Martin.

23

Martin was bone tired when he left Penny Lane, but too hyper to consider sleep. He was still clutching his beeper. He walked through the mall like a stranger. As if he'd never been there before. As if he was lost.

It didn't dawn on him that it was after 9:30 and none of the stores were open. He barely even noticed the customers and sales clerks, anxiously milling about, wondering what had gone wrong.

These were minor details and Martin couldn't be bothered with trivialities. A thousand ideas were pounding on his brain, each clamoring for individual attention.

"There's too much noise here," he said. "I've got to do something about the noise. I have to think. I need absolute silence."

Ascending the stairs to his office, he stopped halfway, in front of a door marked no entry. Martin stood motionless for a moment. He forgot what he wanted to do. Suddenly everything became crystal clear and he entered Garden Park's center of operations. The center of the center.

Martin surveyed the room with the authority of a king. He bent down and examined the rows of dials and switches. A flip of one would cause the sunrise, a flip of another and the garden would be bathed in dew.

"I have the power," he boasted. "I am in control."

He spotted the Beautiful Muzak panel and twisted the knob so hard it came off in his hand. The mall was shrouded in a deafening silence. Martin listened to the void.

"That's better," he said. "Now I can concentrate."

He hurried down to the main level and was instantly seized with a pang of remorse.

"I've tampered with nature," he said. "Forgive me, I have sinned."

Without its muzak, the mall was stripped of its protective covering and stood facing the world, naked and vulnerable. This embarrassed Martin. He blushed at the thought of a nude mall.

Garden Park seemed harsh and obscene. He could hear the polyester writhing, hear the mannequins inject and expel. He looked around at the closed stores, at the bewildered expressions of shoppers and staff.

He was surprised by the sound of his own voice.

"There's no cause for alarm," he said. "If you'll all assemble in the garden, everything will be explained."

The confused patrons willingly obliged. They trusted Martin. He was their leader.

Sandy Rodd and Fair Deal Jake were hidden in the crowd. They didn't want Martin to discover they were keeping an eye on him.

Martin waited until everyone arrived, before mounting his favorite bench.

"Life in a mall is easy," he began, "suffering is missing a sale. I should know. I've never missed any. That's because I live here. I grew up in this mall." He laughed. "You think you grew up here, too. Right? But you didn't. You came here after school or spent Saturdays wandering around. That's all. And that doesn't count. Don't shake your heads. No matter how much time you put in, you never stayed overnight. You always went home. Not me. I never left. Garden Park is my home. I dreamed my dreams here and they all came true. Every evening, after every single store was closed, I used to browse... go anywhere I wanted... play with the latest toys... sleep in 1 of 100 different beds. Oh sure, it was lonely sometimes... Up until yesterday I was always on the lookout for my father. Lincoln O.D., will you ever forgive me? I don't think I appreciated you as much as I do now. You nurtured me. You saw my talent and developed me. You were my parents... my parent corporation. Lincoln O.D., I love you..."

Martin paused and stared at his audience. He didn't care that it dwindled in size. This is good practise for my TV show, he thought.

"A toast," he continued, "to Lincoln Overview... To Garden Park and television... A toast to me. Where's the champagne? Well, it doesn't matter. It's the thought that counts." Martin lifted his arm and pretended to drink from his beeper. "Remember this moment. In a very short time I'm going to be famous. A household name. Are you impressed? You should be. And you'll all be able to say you knew me when... Don't worry, I won't forget you. I'm not like them. They're just retail heathens. They don't realize it was I who allowed them the privilege of being here in the first place. And now they're trying to take everything away from me. Don't let them. Oh please, don't let them..."

Martin was standing on the bench in the middle of the garden, talking to no one. The crowd had dispersed. The muzak was back. It was playing "Elusive Butterfly," Seymour's theme song.

He looked around and noticed a circle of familiar faces walking toward him. He recognized Sandy and Seymour, Edgar and Harry, and Fair Deal Jake.

"Martin," said Seymour, "won't you come down?"

"Everything in a mall has its price!" Martin screamed. "There's no such thing as free-dom..."

"What?" Seymour asked.

"Don't come any closer," Martin said. "Stay where you are." He raised the beeper above his head and flung it to the ground. Before it smashed, it let out a final plaintive beep. "I'm not fooling around. Just get the Lincoln O.D. people on the phone. They'll explain everything. I'm not leaving this mall. Do you hear me? I refuse to go!"

Seymour tried to be soothing. "Nobody's asking you to leave," he said.

"Stop playing games," Martin replied. "I have a lot of work to do today. I'm a very busy person... You can't throw me out on the street. It's unnatural. I hate it there. I won't let you do it. And neither will..."

The rescue group was closing in.

"Call off your army," he said, "or I'll... jump." Martin pointed to the pond below his bench.

Seymour brought them to a halt. "Don't be hasty. We can work this out. Remember yesterday when I told you about immortality? I'm not even sure what that means any more. Maybe you have some suggestions. I'm always willing to listen. But please, stop asking for someone from Lincoln O.D. I own Garden Park now. I closed the deal this morning. That's what I said to the Merchants' Association after you ran out of the meeting."

"You bought Garden Park?" Martin asked.

Seymour nodded.

There was a lump in Martin's throat. "That... That's impossible. No. I don't believe you. You didn't buy it. My father did. He said he would... He promised..."

"I'm not your father."

"I know," Martin replied. "I never thought you were. I was only kidding. It worked pretty well, didn't it?"

"Yes," said Seymour. "It worked very well... Who is your father?"

"The Lincoln O.D. Corporation," Martin announced. "They're not going to let me down. So why don't you go back to your business and I'll take care of mine."

"Look at this," Seymour said. He showed Martin the bill of sale, on Lincoln Overview stationery, stating that effective immediately Isaiah Productions was the new owner and operator of Garden Park.

"No," said Martin. "It can't be..."

"Come down and we can have a nice quiet chat."

"Stay away."

"No one's going to hurt you," Seymour said. "You're still in charge."

"Don't push me," Martin said. "I'll do it... I'm going to... I..."

There was a loud thud as the bench toppled over. Martin had jumped. Unfortunately the brook was only 8 inches deep. He fell on his feet, slipped on the coins and landed face first in the shallow water.

A little boy and his mother walked through the Garden, oblivious to the confusion.

"Go ahead, Billy," said the woman. "This is what you came for."

Obediently, the little boy closed his eyes and threw a coin into the brook. It beaned Martin on the head.

"Beep," said Martin. "Beep... Beep..."

24

After Martin's overextension, as he likes to call it, he was made a ward of the Lincoln Overview Development Corporation. They assumed control over Martin, supervised his recovery and reintroduced him into shopping center life.

They assigned him to a new mall. A plaza on the outskirts of a restful town. The new mall isn't covered and it only has 16 stores. But this is all Martin is able to handle.

It is far enough away that no one recognizes him. He has no past. Like most people, he has become anonymous. He goes about his business and keeps a low profile. He doesn't have a lot of plans.

Sometimes Martin watches Seymour's show on cable TV. He likes it a lot. He feels no bitterness or remorse. And occasionally he'll even get an idea for a sidewalk sale from one of the various guests.

Whenever he passes a discount store's drapery counter, he thinks of Sandy Rodd. He is often tempted to ask for an estimate. But as he has no intention of buying, he feels what's the point.

Peaches is with Martin. She requested the transfer herself. She decided to really watch out for him this time. He hasn't missed an appointment yet.

Every day at 11:30, Martin still experiences the urge to browse. "Old habits die hard," he says.

But because this mall isn't climate-controlled, his browsing has taken on a new dimension. Now he carries an umbrella. He wears an overcoat with pockets full of gloves. He has to pay particular attention to the weather.

Martin doesn't mind.

Once in a while, he misses Garden Park. The excitement, the hustle. He would like to go back. Not permanently, though. For a short visit. But he's been very busy lately and doesn't know when he can find the time.

Without Garden Park, Martin Mall will never be the same. Without Martin Mall, Garden Park will never be any different.